Praise for *Trust Fund Baby*

Douglas Richardson's *American Strays* series is an underground treasure. Books that shuttle between coat pocket and friend's hand like a secret knowledge. And yet, so peculiar, charming, and hilariously funny, the series ought to draw the attention of the mainstream. I loved *The Corruption of Zachary R. Trust Fund Baby* is a brilliant follow-up. If you have not yet discovered the American Strays, make a path, find them. Do it today!

-Richard Bailey, poet

Readers familiar with Richardson's brilliant debut, *The Corruption of Zachary R.*, will be moved yet again by the poignancy of *Trust Fund Baby*. His language moves with the poetic and contemplative movement of a lyric poem as the sorrowful tragedy unfolds of one sheltered boy thrown into a world where he is ill-equipped to deal with the reality of actual human experience.

-Alisa Tangredi, *The Puppet Maker's Bones*

Richardson is a master storyteller, with a great command of the language. The economy of word and raw humanity in his work are astounding.

-Brenda Petrakos

Trust Fund Baby

Douglas Richardson

Weak Creature Press
Los Angeles

Trust Fund Baby
© 2013 by Douglas Richardson
Weak Creature Press
First Printing, February 2013

Library of Congress Control Number: 2013931502
ISBN: 978-0-9842424-5-0

Printed in the United States of America.

Cover design by Heather DeSerio, Precision Edge Design LLC.

Author photo by Prudence Smuggery.

For information on other publications available from Weak Creature Press, please email weakcreature@aol.com.

Contents

PART I

1. Roof Access 3
2. Kay Sunday 5
3. Investigation and Notification.....................6

PART II

4. The Splendorous Layout of Christmas
Morning 11
5. The Negligently Hung Stocking..................13
6. You Think This Is Real, but It Isn't Real at
All..16
7. What's the Idea of Peeing in Our Tub 18
8. Cow with Braces 23
9. Clayton Mulder...25
10. High Octane 29

PART III

11. On Earth as It Is in Heaven.....................33
12. The Heavy Scent of Patchouli 36
13. The Life of a Hurricane............................37
14. Rooster Man..39
15. Religious Education 40
16. Yin/Yang on a Wigwam 43
17. Fancy Clothes and Suffocating Perfume ...44
18. The Rows of Destitute Men 46
19. How Can You Fail to Acknowledge the
Miracle? 48
20. Babylon the Great 51

PART IV

21. Chloe Abadie Reynaud 57
22. From Chloe Blood to Chloe Red................59
23. A Satisfied Man 60

24. Moneybags and Milady 62

PART V

25. The Devil Himself..................................67
26. Three New Friends 68
27. Another Adverse Truth...........................71
28. A Case of Mistaken Identity.....................74
29. My Name Is Vander Stevenson. I Am a Man of God. 76
30. Bon Voyage 78
31. Street Reflection..................................80
32. The Rising Sun 83
33. Heavy Drapes.......................................89
34. Trust Fund Baby....................................91

PART VI

35. Bright Red Swastika...............................97
36. Proper Swastika 98
37. Reconciliation of the Innocents 100
38. No Octane 103
39. Ten Thousand Dollars............................105
40. Pink Cloud, Red Paint...........................110
41. Smug Jimmy 113
42. Top Jimmy..115
43. Charles Larson.....................................118
44. Every Maternal Nerve 121
45. It Can't Be That Dire 123
46. Strong First Impression, but Not a Lasting One 125
47. A Telegram 131

PART VII

48. Two Letters 137
49. Clever and Full of Grace 139
50. Aftermath...141

51. A Scrubs-Clad Woman............................143
52. Fifteenth Birthday 146
53. Harmonious Enough.............................151
54. Her Son's Intensity.............................154
55. A New Car 157
56. Lunch with the Branhoovers 158
57. An Invitation 161
58. A Cryptic Message 163
59. An Inconsequential Lie.........................165
PART VIII
60. From the Ohio to the Mississippi 169
61. You Must Be James.............................170
62. Much Better Than Gasoline Fumes.........172
63. The Worst Thing You've Ever Done.......174
64. The Best Thing That Ever Happened to Me
....179
65. An Inconsequential Lie.........................182
PART IX
66. From the Riverfront Hilton to the Beverly
Hilton 185
67. A Successful Bribe 188
68. A Confession 189
69. A Living Entry 191
70. Eighteenth Birthday 192
71. Divorced...195
72. Six-Thousand-Dollar Promise.................198
73. Dimmed the Light in Their Eyes 200
74. An Adverse Truth and an Inconsequential
Lie..204
75. Rancid Words....................................206
76. Dear Angel 208

For Jen

PART I

1. Roof Access

Haley James Branhoover, the Branhoovers' second son, sat in his room in the youth hostel and wrote the last words of his life—rancid, buttery words that when he read them back aloud, offended him.

"Trust fund baby," he said.

He couldn't stand the sight of his suicide note sitting so accusingly on the nightstand, so he sealed it in the nearest thing he could find: a business reply envelope for *Playboy* magazine.

He went downstairs to the mailroom and dropped the envelope in the slot. On his way back up, he read the words "Roof Access" around each turn of the staircase.

He walked into the open air on the roof. "Roof Access," he said. He repeated the phrase. It gave him unexpected energy.

He sat down on the edge and dangled his legs over.

The youth hostel was only five stories high. H. James Branhoover thought that might not be high enough to kill him, and he didn't want to wind up crippled and in a wheelchair, so he pondered the optimal way to make the plunge onto the concrete below.

He heard the sounds of a television coming from an open window. "This dive has the highest degree of difficulty in the history of the Games," said the announcer. H. James Branhoover let out a burst of sound. A laugh. A sarcastic laugh, certainly, but a laugh nonetheless.

Then more phrases: "Cold beer." "Hot coffee." "Cheeseburger." I want a cheeseburger, he thought.

Then up the street came a homeless man, clutching his mangled hand and humming Haydn. It was the man from the alley who reminded him of Charles Larson. Searchlights crossed overhead. A soft breeze moved his arm hairs. He closed his eyes and pushed himself off the roof.

Several minutes later, the homeless man arrived at the spot where the lifeless body of H. James Branhoover lay. He reached out his injured hand and touched the corpse. "I am afraid to die," he said.

2. Kay Sunday

A strand of Kay Sunday's long blonde hair dangled from the notebook of H. James Branhoover. "Church blonde. Mother hen blonde," it read. "Pretty blonde. Wholesome. Winsome. Helpful." But, like any two people who have known each other for a long time, she had betrayed him, and he had betrayed her.

Kay Sunday was slight of build, had large, pale blue eyes, and the highly unglamorous habit of sniffing gasoline fumes for fun. She hung out with a group of innocents who made you feel your age when in their presence; that your desires were silly and why not try to relax. Sit on a porch and decompress. Do something real and worthwhile, something unpolitical, like planting roses.

Kay Sunday was H. James Branhoover's best friend.

3. Investigation and Notification

Because H. James Branhoover had mailed his suicide note to the subscription processing center for *Playboy* magazine in Boulder, Colorado, the detectives in charge of the investigation of his death were initially unable to rule out accident or homicide.

They placed the strand of Kay Sunday's hair in a plastic bag and scrutinized each entry of his notebook for possible clues.

They questioned the homeless man from the alley who had reminded H. James Branhoover of Charles Larson, as well as one of the boys who fake gayness for the sake of slavery, who saw the homeless man reaching for the body and muttering "I am afraid to die."

It would have taken expert detective work, or even clairvoyance, to uncover the connection the homeless man had to H. James Branhoover. Fortunately for all involved, the detectives did not possess such powers.

Eventually the suicide note was found and the investigation closed. Mrs. Branhoover received the news of her second son's suicide in the comfort of her Colonial mansion in Pittsburgh, where she spends her days beneath the drapes of the living room window, looking at the river below.

PART II

4. The Splendorous Layout of Christmas Morning

Energy shot through the five-year-old body of H. James Branhoover—the second son of H. Charles Branhoover and Chloe Branhoover— as he lay in bed with a nauseated sense of anticipation of what awaited him that Christmas morning.

Jimmy's bedroom was the lone occupied room of six on the second floor of the Branhoovers' two-story, ten-bedroom Colonial mansion located on the summit of one of Pittsburgh's many hills.

Jimmy Branhoover was a little prince living in a castle at the top of the world, the Allegheny River below serving as his moat.

His father, the well-to-do and good-for-nothing banker H. Charles Branhoover, was the aging king, now in his seventies, feeble and mildly ashamed of the totality of his life.

His mother, Mrs. Chloe Branhoover, the unlikely queen, the former roughhouse prostitute Chloe Red, had recently celebrated her fortieth birthday, which meant that mother was as close in age to her second son as she was to her husband.

The Branhoovers' first son, Bernard, of whom Jimmy was entirely unaware, was employed as a concierge in a bed-and-breakfast on a road called Bath in a seaside village out West. Bernard Branhoover, who changed his name to Bernrd Red to promote the sensation of being hit in the head with a rock, had not been in contact with his parents since his father had expelled him from Pittsburgh when Bernrd was eighteen. He was now twenty-five and, like Jimmy, was unaware that he had a brother.

So the home of the ignorant little prince was permeated by the scent of the Christmas tree (a twenty-foot Douglas fir) and the electricity that lit the lights in its branches seemed the same electricity that lit young Jimmy when he opened his bedroom door Christmas morning and beheld the splendorous layout of presents, two dozen, all his, and the lone stocking, also his, hanging directly above the well-mannered fire in the Branhoovers' fireplace.

5. The Negligently Hung Stocking

Jimmy Branhoover rushed down the stairs and fell face-first into the plush carpet of the living room, where all the excitement of Christmas had been arranged.

His parents, who had been awaiting their son's arrival for the past half hour, sprang to their feet in anticipation of their son's crying, which, to their surprise, failed to manifest. The severity of the fall was sufficient to cause a minor concussion, but the boy seemed completely unfazed. The splendor of the two dozen presents, all his, trumped the jolting pain inside his skull.

Jimmy bounced across the carpet with the awkward precision of a pouncing kitten and sat among his presents under the Christmas tree.

His mother, feeling guilty about her violent reign over her first son, doted on Jimmy as her penance, which seemed to explain the boy's exuberant and unassuming disposition.

But Mrs. Chloe Branhoover had also, of late, resumed her role as Chloe Red. Not only was her husband old, but he was also cheap and controlling. As a banker, he believed the only way to keep his young, formerly wayward wife securely in his possession was to restrict her allowance. But tightening his purse strings did nothing but loosen his wife's legs and her attention to detail on this particular Christmas morning.

Mrs. Branhoover had haphazardly wrapped Jimmy's gifts and inconsistently marked the tags. Sure enough, eighteen gifts were marked "To:

Jimmy, From: Santa," but three gifts read "To: Jimmy, From: Chloe," two gifts read "To: Jimmy, From: blank line," and one gift read "To: Bernard, From: Santa."

When Jimmy read "To: Bernard," his faced twisted mildly, but then he burst out laughing. "Look, Mom and Dad," he said, pointing at the tag. "Santa accidentally gave one of this kid Bernard's presents to me!"

Then, just as H. James Branhoover, the Branhoovers' second son, began tearing into the wrapping paper of their first son's present, the overstuffed stocking above the fireplace, which Chloe Red had negligently hung with a piece of masking tape, dropped onto the hearth below, scattering the contents into the fire, which began to rage with the new fuel of Jimmy's toys. Now their son seemed finally to notice the pain inside his skull and began to cry inconsolably. Mother and father looked at each other with accusatory eyes and then descended upon their five-year-old boy, smothering him with the overzealous affection of secretive and lying parents whose consciences had condemned them long ago.

6. You Think This Is Real, but It Isn't Real at All

Jimmy Branhoover was still a pouncing kitten the following fall, when he entered kindergarten at the very private, formerly traditional, and now progressive Carden School.

While some of the children cried and clung to their parents on the first day of school, this was not the case for Jimmy or the slight, blonde girl, Kay Sunday, who, even at the age of five, had otherworldly eyes that said she knew something you didn't.

The Carden School, from day one, employed its newfangled approach to education and sat "like with like" rather than "name with name," which meant that it was possible for a "B" to sit next to an "S," which meant that Jimmy and Kay, whom the teacher determined to be like with like, were seated next to each other.

While the two children's personalities weren't exactly alike, there was no disputing their mutual affection.

By the third day of school, the entire class had been arranged according to the teacher's intuition. The exuberant and unassuming Jimmy and the alien Kay were already best friends who shared everything, including the same palette for their finger paints, which Jimmy, without hesitation or reservation, ran through Kay's hair.

Kay Sunday's hair looked like a hallucination, with purple, red, and green streaks to complement her natural blonde.

The teacher, Mrs. Germany, Deirdre to her husband and the other teachers, upon seeing Kay's hair, momentarily forgot her forward-looking ideology and grabbed Jimmy by the arm.

"Jimmy!" she exclaimed. "Don't ever paint Kay's hair again! Understand?"

Jimmy Branhoover was stunned silent by his teacher's sudden rage, but not Kay Sunday. Little Kay looked directly at Mrs. Germany with her otherworldly eyes and said, "You think this is real, but it isn't real at all." Then Kay ran her hand through her painted hair, smeared it on Jimmy's shirt and then her own shirt.

The paint seemed real enough to Mrs. Germany.

7. What's the Idea of Peeing in Our Tub

By the time Halloween came around, Jimmy Branhoover and Kay Sunday were inseparable, inasmuch as is possible for a couple of kindergarteners to be.

Mrs. Germany, the progressive kindergarten teacher, was so charmed by the two children—and by her self-satisfaction that she and her pedagogical philosophy had been responsible for bringing them together—that she suggested to Jimmy's and Kay's parents at the October PTA meeting that the two should spend the night together, which she promptly restated as "they should have a sleepover" when Mrs. Branhoover slapped her across the face.

Mr. and Mrs. Sunday, who, unlike the Branhoovers, were accustomed to being and doing everything together, including sharing their unlikely family business as spiritual consultants and amateur astronomers, selling God and telescopes, immediately assented to the idea, volunteering the Branhoovers' mansion for the occasion.

Mrs. Branhoover, unaccompanied by her septuagenarian husband, glared at the Sundays and vowed to hate them and their dubious business forever. "Will this Saturday night be good for Kay?" she muttered. "Saturday is Halloween."

Mr. and Mrs. Sunday looked at each other, their eyes beaming vacuously, yet infectiously, and then they looked at the sullen Mrs. Branhoover and blurted out in unison, "Oh, how you shine."

Now Mrs. Branhoover was beside herself. "Bring Kay over by three o'clock so we can dress them up for Halloween," she said, and then quickly turned and walked away.

* * * * *

The Sundays arrived at the Branhoovers' door at 3:25 that Saturday. Kay had her costume curled up in both arms. It was a bee costume, complete with two bee wings, six bee legs, and black and gold bee makeup.

Mrs. Branhoover let Kay inside and pointed toward the living room. "Go wait in that room and I'll get Jimmy," she said. Then she looked at Mr. and Mrs. Sunday and instructed them to return the next morning at ten to pick up their daughter.

By the time Mrs. Branhoover had closed the front door and turned around, Jimmy had found Kay.

Jimmy was already in costume. Mrs. Branhoover, as an experiment, had picked three superhero costumes: Superman, Batman, and Wonder Woman. Jimmy immediately picked Batman. While she was alarmed that her son chose the Dark Knight (yet not really that surprised, given who his father and brother were), at least he didn't choose Wonder Woman, which pacified her fear that she had given birth to a sissy, what with him palling around with a girl and all.

Batman and the bumblebee frolicked in the living room smearing the gold bee makeup on each other, while Mrs. Branhoover looked on without an inkling of concern or amusement.

As for Mr. Branhoover, he chose to remain in his bedroom, too tired to contend with the frenetic energy of two children on Halloween.

At six o'clock Mrs. Branhoover took the kids trick-or-treating and by seven had them back and preparing for bed.

Jimmy bathed first and was already in bed. Mr. Branhoover, having forgotten that there were two children in his home that night, opened the bathroom door and was shocked to see little Kay sitting in a bathtub of golden water.

Mr. Branhoover blurted out, "What's the idea of peeing in our tub?!" To which Kay, giggling, responded, "It's not my pee. It's bee pee."

Mr. Branhoover slammed the door shut and returned to his bedroom. As he laid his head on his pillow, he allowed a barely audible, breathy chuckle to escape his old lungs.

8. Cow with Braces

Kindergarten for Jimmy and Kay went by in a timeless hallucination of finger paint. Timeless in the sense that time, and the dread that comes with its passing, had no influence on the two children.

So the school year came to an end and the summer passed by, too, which meant it was the autumn of first grade.

Jimmy thought the first-grade classroom smelled like a pumpkin cloud and resembled the big kids' classrooms because it had cursive letters written on the blackboard.

Jimmy and Kay's first-grade teacher was the same as their kindergarten teacher—Mrs. Germany.

Mrs. Germany was pleased to see that Jimmy and Kay were still friends with the same enthusiasm as the previous year. She knew firsthand how a summer together (or a summer apart) can change the dynamic of a friendship.

She looked out the window, thinking wistful thoughts of friendships come and gone and of the heartbreak of change.

Then, in the way that only a mature adult can do, she banished the memories of a lifetime and returned her focus to her responsibility: the twenty-two children waiting for first grade to begin.

Mrs. Germany faced the class, smiled purposefully, and asked, "Do any of my returning students notice anything different about me this year?" Kay Sunday thrust her hand high above her head, waving in that same hand a large piece of construction paper, which Mrs. Germany took from the girl and examined.

Then, in the way that only a mature adult can do, Mrs. Germany banished her hurt feelings and held up the drawing that Kay had produced in her first minutes in the first grade: a cow with braces.

Mrs. Germany grinned widely and the classroom burst out laughing. "That's right, Kay Sunday. I got braces this summer," she said.

Kay was proud of her achievement, but she was perplexed by the laughter. Mrs. Germany could see that Kay honestly meant no harm, and so laughed herself.

9. Clayton Mulder

With the exception of the straightening of Mrs. Germany's crooked teeth, the eight seasons of the first and second grades came and went with few perceptible changes. The same twenty-two students progressed through their lessons at the expected rates, and the relationships established in kindergarten persisted.

But then came the autumn of the third grade, and with it the arrival of a twenty-third student: Clayton Mulder.

Clay Mulder had moved to Pittsburgh from Santa Cruz, California, on account of his father's procuring a lucrative administrative position at the Presbyterian hospital.

Clay had spent the first eight years of his life on a boogie board in the chilly, shark-infested water of Northern California, and among the redwoods and deadheads who were his parents' friends. As such, he was an affable, willing, and fearless boy, and a natural to become friends with Kay and Jimmy.

Clay deflected with charm and ease Kay and Jimmy's early and obvious attempt to make fun of his name, which he said he planned to change as soon as the law permitted. When Kay asked him what he was going to change it to, he jokingly said Millicent. All three of them laughed, and then Jimmy, who had misheard him, asked,

"Why would you want to be called Innocent?" They all laughed again.

Kay seemed to go into a trance. "I like it," she said. "I really like it. I'm going to start calling you that now, if you don't mind. I mean, my real last name is Sutter, so it's no big deal."

"I'm good with that," said Clay Mulder. "Kay Sunday and the Innocents. That would be a cool band name."

"Definitely," said Jimmy.

"Jimmy, you could be Innocent #1, and I'll be Innocent #2," said Clay, who walked over to the supply cabinet, removed a bottle of rubber cement, unscrewed the lid, and took a deep whiff. "Let's celebrate," he said, passing the bottle to Jimmy, who glanced at it and then passed it to Kay, who, to Jimmy's surprise, also took a deep whiff.

"It's so strange you did that," said Kay to Innocent #2. "I found a gas can on my porch at home, and I really like the smell of the gas," she said.

27

"We should partake of the gasoline fumes after school," said Innocent #2. "That'll be the start of Kay Sunday and the Innocents."

"Yes!" exclaimed Kay. "There's some stuff I'd like to get off my chest about my parents' church, and this could be perfect for that."

Jimmy nodded, trying his best to muster enthusiasm.

"When do we convene the first session?" asked Innocent #2.

"Let's meet after school next Monday," said Kay. "There are some preparations I'd like to make, so we are sure to do this right."

"Sounds good to me," said Innocent #2.

"Me too," said Jimmy, reluctantly.

10. High Octane

The following Monday afternoon, Kay Sunday, Jimmy Branhoover, and Innocent #2 convened on Kay's porch for the inaugural meeting of Kay Sunday and the Innocents.

Kay had gone to great lengths to prepare the porch in a manner consistent with the principles of her parents' religion. She had placed three wicker chairs facing each other in a triangular formation and the gas can in the exact center of the triangle. Forming a circle around the triangle of chairs was a wreath of potted roses. The three of them sat in their assigned chairs, and then Kay spoke:

"The nature of these sessions is likely to be political, involving unfortunate truths of human controversy. For this reason, I have surrounded us with roses and placed the healing fumes of gasoline within easy reach. Upon commencement of each session, I suggest that we pass the can around twice, and then testify fearlessly and honestly about the matters that concern us. Innocent #1, I understand your reluctance to inhale the fumes, so there will be no judgment or reprisal should you decide to refrain. Do either of you have any questions?"

Neither boy spoke.

"Okay," said Kay. "For this inaugural session, I recommend that we sit in silence and consider the roses surrounding us, how they are just as real and worthwhile—and perhaps more humane— than any human controversy."

Kay Sunday and the Innocents sat in silence for five minutes, and then Kay adjourned the meeting.

Jimmy spent that evening in his bedroom, feeling uneasy about the new ritual of the high-octane sessions and anxious about the changing dynamic of his friendship with Kay Sunday.

PART III

11. On Earth as It Is in Heaven

The Sundays (legally, the Sutters), Mr. and Mrs., Kristov and Kristina, Kris and Kris, were spiritual consultants and amateur astronomers, selling God and telescopes. Their slogan was "On earth as it is in heaven." And, to illustrate their point, they would often say, "A hurricane is more than a hurricane. A galaxy is less than a galaxy."

The Sundays were poor. Then they were rich. Then they were poor again. But their daughter, Kay, was bright and happy, and she believed in her parents' brand of religion wholeheartedly, never a question asked. It was as if Kay were the living proof of the veracity of their vision. The Sundays believed in intelligent design and that there was consistency throughout the universe. "On earth as it is in heaven" and "what you loose on earth is loosed in heaven."

The Sundays took this literally and as their primary directive. Their one-room church on the outskirts of Pittsburgh (near an Amish community, which thought the Sundays were members of some kind of cult) had a wooden cross on the roof, but that was already there when the Sundays bought the property. The church was painted a spacey, deep purple. The outside west wall had a perfectly rendered solar system painted on it, while the outside east wall had the Milky Way galaxy on one half and a hurricane on the other half.

The roof was partially retractable because the Sundays' church was more an observatory than a house of worship. On clear nights the roof would open and the Sundays' prize possession, a NASA-quality telescope—which nearly plunged them into bankruptcy—would announce its presence.

The Sundays got many converts, but most were not religious zealots. Rather, they were fledgling astronomers who quickly wearied of the whole God angle.

A pattern was established: new converts in; then a month of preaching and stargazing would pass, with the converts becoming ever more annoyed by the preaching. Some would quit the congregation. Mr. Sunday would attempt to convince the remaining converts to stay, his faith never wavering. His appeal would usually go something like this: "If you read into Maya, ancient Egypt, and ancient Greek history and their knowledge of astronomy, you'll find that life on earth has a symbiotic relationship with the cosmos. For example, the birth of Jesus with the brightest star. What I'm trying to impart is that God is in the distant cosmos. This is true. Also true: You are the distant cosmos and God is in you. Hear the good news!"

The Sundays' spacey church would soon be empty, except for the telescope.

12. The Heavy Scent of Patchouli

Kay Sunday and the Innocents sniffed high-octane fumes and testified.

Kay: A thin man in a short-sleeved, button-up shirt was handing out Jesus brochures. I didn't see them, but I knew they were Jesus brochures because the heavy scent of patchouli preceded the man. That's the way things work, in case you didn't know. True knowledge comes naturally like that. The knowledge that comes from reason, have you ever noticed how it always winds up being disproved?

Innocent #2: Rings so true that Jesus must have struck the bell himself from the brightest star!

Kay: Testify, Innocent #2.

Innocent #2: I saw that same thin man the other day. I was on my skateboard and I was in a hurry. I had a determined expression on my face, which the man must have found inspiring. When

I rolled by him, he clapped his hands and said, "God bless you." So I said, "Shut up."

Kay: Good for you, Innocent #2. Now, I believe in Jesus as much as the next man, but that was just meddlesome.

13. The Life of a Hurricane

Mrs. Sunday wrote a sermon, which she recited at the beginning of every service. It went like this:

Summertime arrives in the tropics. The air warms over the water. The sea creatures also pick up the pace, diving down, darting up, and round and round the schools go the sharks. Water spouts swirl and the spiral forms. Category One has just been born.

Category Two, the adolescent storm, cocky, unstable, unsure of itself, drifts rebellious over the sea and soon becomes a Category Three.

Category Four: Ladies, fat and loud, gossip around the rotund table. Let them go. Don't be proud.

Category Five: The Wall of Sound.

Denouement: It's raining in Arkansas.

The congregation would just sit there, dumbfounded, thinking, There is a cross on the roof of this church, isn't there?

14. Rooster Man

Kay Sunday and the Innocents sniffed high-octane fumes and testified.

Kay: A rooster man came strutting down the street in a fancy suit. He cut across the park with folks in shorts and T-shirts sitting in the green grass with picnic baskets, and I thought, A man's got no business walking through a park in a fancy suit unless he's a preacher. And I've never met a rooster man who was a preacher, at least not a respectable preacher transmitting Jesus from the cosmos. A man strutting in a fancy suit must have something to hide.

Innocent #1: God bless you, Kay Sunday.

Innocent #2: I saw that same rooster man the other day up to the same no-good thing, and I thought, You come into this world and you don't know a thing, and then one day—or over a week, maybe—you figure out about death, and once you've done that, once you understand that the day will come when you no longer know the back of your own hand, you know there's just no good reason to be strutting around like a rooster in a fancy suit.

Kay: Innocent #2, you are transmitting!

Innocent #1: God bless you, Innocent #2.

15. Religious Education

Despite the secular philosophy of the Carden School, Jimmy was receiving a thorough religious education as a result of his close relationship with the Sundays, the high-octane sessions with Kay and Innocent #2, and through his mother, who was unwittingly exposing her son to the Book of Revelation.

When Jimmy turned eight, Chloe Branhoover, worn down by her life as a roughhouse prostitute and her sham of a marriage, discovered the televangelists, whom she watched in a room on the second floor across from Jimmy's room after her husband went to bed.

Chloe Red was usually able to muster a half hour of attention before falling asleep on the sofa.

The televangelists preached all night long until the morning news came on at six, which meant that the family member who received the message was young Jimmy, who drifted in and out of consciousness, hearing verses such as "I am the Alpha and the Omega, who is, and who was, and who is come, the Almighty" and "He will rule them with an iron scepter; he will dash them to pieces like pottery" and "Behold, I come like a thief! Blessed is he who stays awake and keeps his clothes with him, so that he may not go naked and be shamefully exposed." In summary, the message he received was this: Forces are aligning and the end is near, cryptic and terrifying.

The profound impact that such a message can have on an eight-year-old who recently had the characteristics of a pouncing kitten cannot be underestimated.

Over the span of a single month, Jimmy Branhoover the pouncing kitten became Jimmy Branhoover the brooding Christian with Book of Revelation doomsday scenarios running through his mind day and night.

Chloe Branhoover, whom Jimmy began to think of as Babylon the Great, panicked over the abrupt change in her son's personality. She brought him to a psychiatrist, who dubiously recommended that he also speak with a priest. The hope was that a religious man would be able to shed light on the meaning of the final book of the Bible. And that is exactly what the priest did, which made Jimmy even more of a true believer.

Suddenly Mrs. Branhoover missed her first son. She could comprehend Bernrd Red promoting the sensation of being hit in the head with a rock. She was utterly perplexed by her second son, the eight-year-old doomsday preacher.

16. Yin/Yang on a Wigwam

Kay Sunday and the Innocents sniffed high-octane fumes and testified.

Kay: A heretic wearing a gold watch and stinking of patchouli oil bought an acre across the road from my parents' church. I saw the man sitting on a brand new tree stump, a hot chainsaw resting on his lap and a newly fallen pine lying in the green on his left, its spirit hovering in the dust. And do you know what that man was doing?

Innocent #1: Testify, Kay Sunday.

Kay: He was wiggling his leg, that's what he was doing.

Innocent #1: Only a pervert wiggles his leg.

Innocent #2: I saw that leg-wiggling pervert the other day. I saw him on his acre painting a yin/yang symbol on a wigwam.

Innocent #1: Only a heretic would paint a yin/yang on a wigwam.

Kay: What a charlatan that man is! The Reverend Patchouli Goldwatch! That's what his name is. I don't care what he says otherwise.

17. Fancy Clothes and Suffocating Perfume

Kay Sunday and the Innocents sniffed high-octane fumes and testified.

Kay: The overwhelming scent of patchouli blew with the breeze across the road and invaded our church, so I went to have a chat with the Reverend Patchouli Goldwatch.

Innocent #1: Set him straight, Kay Sunday!

Kay: When I looked him in the eye, I recognized him as the meddlesome thin man handing out Jesus brochures and interfering with Innocent #2's skateboard, and also as the rooster man in a fancy suit strutting across the park, ruining picnics. I looked him in the eye, and he said, "My name is Vander Stevenson. I am a man of God."

Innocent #2: The first words out of the man's mouth are a lie!

Kay: That's the truth, Innocent #2. He's all fancy clothes and suffocating perfume, but he's not a man of God.

Innocent #2: I'll bet he was wiggling his leg while he was looking you in the eye and lying.

Kay: I should have known to look, but I didn't. That would've given him away for sure.

18. The Rows of Destitute Men

When H. James Branhoover was alone in his room reading the Book of Revelation, his ideas were big and his thoughts profound. He grew fortified in his biblical solitude. He constructed entire world-changing sermons in his head with words so powerful that he feared for the lives of those who might hear them, thrust from the comfort (or discomfort) of their daily existences and into prophecy-fulfilling action.

He vowed late at night that the next morning he would rise up in the light and save a man or two out in the street.

He would walk down to the Salvation Army thrift store, where the men stood fidgeting in filthy rows, and his eyes would fall upon them with a mixture of compassion, pity, and condescension. His mind and heart would swell with anxious fury as he searched for the words that seemed so true and large in the safety of his bedroom, but now seemed shamefully small against the intimidating faces of the day.

H. James Branhoover would walk past the rows of destitute men in silence and wind up over at Kay Sunday's, where, as Innocent #1, he would continue to be silent except when he praised Kay and Innocent #2 for their high-octane outbursts—which he knew were not as important as his nocturnes—and all the attendant humiliation of knowing that he was bringing his Kay and Innocent #2 together.

19. How Can You Fail to Acknowledge the Miracle?

Every day for a week, Jimmy walked down the hill to the Salvation Army thrift store, where he passed by the rows of destitute men. He felt on the verge of saying something profound to them, but he intuitively understood the more days that passed, the less likely he would be to say anything at all.

After the third time Jimmy came into their realm, the men began to talk to one another about the boy who carried the burgundy Bible.

The honest man, whose only vices were Rolling Rock and Tanqueray, thought Jimmy was some sort of delirium tremens angel and hoped he wouldn't ever speak and shatter the illusion.

The quiet man with the permanent scowl—the kind of man who shuns his mother because she brought him into the world—thought Jimmy was put there by the FBI as bait, though he would never get into specifics. The quiet man muttered "Damien Freakshow" whenever Jimmy passed by.

And then there was the self-proclaimed "inveterate grifter," whom the quiet man, under his breath, called the "inveterate incompetent." This man thought Jimmy smelled of wealthy parents and began to plot a way to get him to bring money along with his Bible.

* * * * *

So late at night the young H. James Branhoover studied the Book of Revelation and rehearsed his sermons for the rows of destitute men down at the Salvation Army thrift store.

After several trips down the hill, Jimmy had completely lost his nerve and had begun to use the time to consider other, less risky, forms of service to God and mankind.

Nevertheless, he walked again among the intimidating faces, but this time the quiet man with the permanent scowl nudged Jimmy hard enough to knock the Bible out of his grasp and onto the concrete. As Jimmy bent down to pick it up, the quiet man blurted out "Damien Freakshow!"

The inveterate grifter's tongue darted in and out of his tight lips and he wrung his hands.

The honest man cringed and backed up against the wall.

Meanwhile, the quiet man again knocked the Bible out of Jimmy's grasp, but this time Jimmy stared the man down and shouted, "How can you fail to acknowledge the miracle?" The quiet man withered as if he had been doused in holy water, and the honest man came off the wall laughing and applauding his angel.

20. Babylon the Great

The Holy Spirit had moved H. James Branhoover. There was no other plausible explanation. He pored over all of his sermons and his notes when he returned home, and nowhere did he find that preemptive strike of a question: "How can you fail to acknowledge the miracle?" He relived the moment over and over in his bedroom—evil had withered and good had blossomed because he was there and had spoken the truth: "How can you fail to acknowledge the miracle?"

Just then his mother burst into his room, a John in tow. "Jimmy, this is Clarence," she said. "Clarence owes us money, so he's going to take us in your father's car to Target to buy us some things."

Neither of the two young men spoke as H. Charles Branhoover's BMW wound its way down the hill and out into the suburbs to Target, where the irritated Chloe Red yanked a shopping cart from the back of the shopping cart train and thrust it in the direction of Clarence the John, who pushed the cart up and down the aisles while Chloe tossed items into the cart with one hand and crushed her son's bicep with the other hand.

Clarence couldn't help but notice Jimmy wincing in pain. "Hey, no need to take this out on the boy," he said. "It's not his fault I was short. I could've sworn I had another hundred in my wallet."

"You probably did, Clarence," said Jimmy. "My mom's a hooker, you know. She probably rifled through your pants and took it when you weren't paying attention."

Chloe Red smacked her son across the face and dragged him out of the store, leaving Clarence with the cart and wondering about his money.

* * * * *

The next morning, Chloe Branhoover wasted no time in removing Jimmy from the Carden School. She wanted to punish him twofold: by separating him from Kay Sunday and by homeschooling him in the manner of her first son, Bernard.

PART IV

21. Chloe Abadie Reynaud

Unlike most orphans, Chloe Abadie Reynaud was a noisy, active child, easy to laugh and to make others laugh. She was extroverted and rough. Girls were intimidated by her energy and her fearlessness around bugs and animals, and later around older boys and men.

And, like most forces of nature, Chloe Abadie Reynaud produced a wide swath of destruction. She seemed a victim of her own energy, to wit:

Chloe was fond of playing "smear the queer" with the boys during recess, a brutal and exhilarating kind of football involving a dozen or so boys (and Chloe), in which the object was to give the ball to one boy and for this boy to run for his life as the other boys tried to tackle him.

Smear the queer was a difficult game for the teachers to comprehend, and they often broke it up thinking a fight had started.

But for the boys in Chloe's age group, running and hitting and being hit was a thrilling and mandatory antidote to stultifying school.

One morning, shortly after her tenth birthday, Chloe woke with stomach cramps. All she could think about was 10:30 recess, when she could take out her suffering on the boys on the field.

The 10:30 bell rang and Chloe ran to the ball bin, grabbing the football and dashing out onto the grass, where she taunted the boys, whom she somehow knew would never have to suffer the way she was suffering now.

The boys charged onto the playground, but Chloe, rather than elude them, picked the biggest boy and ran directly at him. The ensuing collision was life-altering for both children.

Chloe dropped as if she had collided with a gorilla. Worse, she began to sob as the menstrual blood trickled down her thighs.

The biggest boy initially thought Chloe had been mortally wounded and began waving at the teachers for help. Chloe leapt to her feet and slammed the biggest boy's chest. "Stop it!" she yelled.

The bell rang. As the children dispersed, murmurs of "Chloe Blood" could be heard on the playground and in the halls.

22. From Chloe Blood to Chloe Red

The evolution from Chloe Blood to Chloe Red was a predictable one. By the time grade school came to an end, Chloe had no friends, but that didn't diminish her noise or energy, which she redirected toward the more challenging demographic of older boys and men.

Her grades, which were never spectacular in grade school, began to suffer all the more when, at the age of fourteen, she unhesitatingly agreed to enter into an agreement with an enterprising high school boy whereby Chloe would let the boy touch her in increasingly dangerous places in exchange for increasing sums of money.

The arrangement proved so successful for Chloe that she mysteriously began to attract older and older, richer and richer clients, the oldest and richest of whom, fifty-one-year-old H. Charles Branhoover, touched Chloe Red in the most dangerous of places, so dangerous, in fact, that the sum of money required in compensation set up Chloe and her offspring for life.

23. A Satisfied Man

From the age of three, H. Charles Branhoover was a satisfied man. Never a child. Never given to boyish whims. Shrewd. Self-centered. Never too short. Never too tall. Always stronger than average. An aggressive dog. A bloodhound. Always in the lead without the slightest pity or compunction for the weak creatures of the world, including his wife and two sons, whom he took care of (financed and kept hidden) strictly out of utilitarian self-interest.

He really couldn't be bothered with what he considered to be the by-product of his lust, which was prodigious.

H. Charles Branhoover carried himself with dignity, had aristocratic mores, and because he was utterly amoral, had a nose for money like a bloodhound has a nose for fox. H. Charles Branhoover was an ideal American.

It wasn't until he attained seventy years, when his mind and body finally weakened, that he began to exhibit that most un-American of character traits—self-reflection.

This new self-reflection was the direct and proximate cause of his new feebleness and his mild shame over the totality of his life.

He began to notice churches, for example. He began to visit cemeteries.

He began to wonder about the whereabouts of his first son, Bernard, or perhaps more accurately, whether Bernard was real or a figment of his fledgling imagination.

24. Moneybags and Milady

H. Charles Branhoover and his wife raised Jimmy like a prince, but while a princely upbringing is filled with physical comfort and ease, and the occasional anonymous servant, the mental aspect is less certain.

Outside of his relationship with Kay Sunday, Jimmy had little in the way of human companionship. When he wasn't at school, Jimmy was lonely and frightened, spending most of his home life trying to stay out of the way of his parents.

With his father, this really wasn't so difficult. Father and son spent most of their days sequestered in their rooms, which were on different floors of the mansion, and when the two did cross each other's paths, Mr. Branhoover looked at Jimmy like he was someone he should know but couldn't place the name with the face.

Jimmy's mother was more of a challenge.

Mr. Branhoover was essentially a wraith haunting the halls of the mansion, which was less than satisfying for Mrs. Branhoover, who continued to entertain gentleman visitors. Jimmy was forced to vie for his mother's attention with the dregs of humanity, white-collar types with high incomes and low scruples.

Jimmy was frustrated by his mother's distance and her darting eyes. He despised his mother's clientele, who had three reactions to his presence: overfriendly, outright dismissive, or oddly mortified by him, as if he were some sort of fatal microbe. Jimmy despised them, but he also took their behavior to heart and, on occasion, unintentionally disrespected himself by showing them his good report cards and school artwork. To their credit, most of these men were one-time customers, their desperate horniness trumped by shameful compassion for the little boy.

Worse for Jimmy than his encounters with his mother's guests, however, were his encounters with his parents on those rare occasions when the three of them were together in the same room. The antipathy mother and father had for each other was palpable. Jimmy noticed that they rarely called each other by their real names, but by made-up names that he could tell they disliked. Mr. Branhoover, when perturbed, called Mrs. Branhoover "Milady," and Mrs. Branhoover, with an utter lack of art, called her husband "Moneybags." When the perturbation was particularly acute, Mr. Branhoover would say, "Once a whore, always a whore," to which Mrs. Branhoover would respond, "Look who's talking."

PART V

25. The Devil Himself

Kay Sunday and the Innocents sniffed high-octane fumes and testified.

Kay: Vander Stevenson, aka meddlesome thin man, aka death-dissing, leg-wiggling, picnic-ruining, yin/yang-painting, land-grabbing, church-stealing rooster man, aka the Reverend Patchouli Goldwatch, needs to be straightened out.

Innocent #1: Testify, Kay Sunday.

Kay: The godless reverend has been attending my parents' services on the sly. He's been mocking our faith right inside the doors of our church. He snickered at my mom's sermon on the topic of hurricanes. The man wants nothing less than our parishioners, our land, our church, and our telescope.

Innocent #2: Patchouli Goldwatch is the Devil himself!

Kay: Amen, Innocent #2. [Kay embraces Innocent #2. Innocent #1 frowns.]

Kay: Innocent #1, are you okay? This is good news. We've identified the Devil in our midst.

Innocent #1: Bless you, Kay Sunday. Let's bring the Devil down.

Kay looked at the gas can, wondering at the efficacy of its contents.

26. Three New Friends

Devastated by Kay's enthusiastic embrace of Innocent #2, H. James Branhoover did not go home that night.

Instead, he walked down to the Salvation Army thrift store in search of his three new friends.

He walked recklessly along the filthy row, not quite able to make out the faces in the dark.

"Hey, Damien Freakshow, where's your Bible?" asked the quiet man, breaking the silence.

Jimmy shrugged and replied, "I must have left it next to the gas can."

"You weren't going to burn it, were you, Angel?" asked the honest man.

"I didn't have a lighter," replied Jimmy.

The inveterate grifter giggled through his tight lips and darting tongue.

"How can you fail to acknowledge the miracle?" said the quiet man.

Jimmy laughed and joined them. The honest man carefully wrapped his angel with a wool blanket.

* * * * *

Several hours passed in silence and sound, in wakefulness and unconsciousness, under the sun and the moon, for the new young man and his three new friends.

For the first time in his eleven years, H. James Branhoover had mentally accepted an adverse truth: Kay Sunday didn't love him, even though she knew he loved her.

He sat with his three friends, similarly unloved, and felt simultaneously burgeoning camaraderie and creeping bitterness.

This was different from his parents not loving him. He was okay with that because he didn't really care for them either. There was, in fact, a certain security in their mutual lack of affection.

But this was different. Jimmy accepted that Kay didn't love him, but he didn't accept that he couldn't change her mind.

The sermons in H. James Branhoover's notebook would now have to share space with strategies for winning back Kay Sunday.

27. Another Adverse Truth

H. James Branhoover didn't arrive home until late the next afternoon, which meant he had missed school, which meant his mother had actually noticed his absence, since she was his new teacher.

It would be unfair, however, to say that Chloe Red didn't love her boy. She did. And she was determined to demonstrate her love when she saw him stumble through the front door, the telltale scent of "the night before" in his clothes.

"Jimmy," said Chloe Branhoover to her second son as he began the dazed ascent to his bedroom. He twitched and, without turning, continued climbing.

"Haley James Branhoover!" she yelled. "Get back down here this instant."

For a brief moment, Jimmy wondered if he had wandered into the wrong house, or his house but in an alternate universe.

His mother had never used his full name before, and Jimmy thought it odd that he sort of liked hearing it said this way. He'd heard other parents (including Kay's parents) call their children by their whole names when he was at the Carden School, but never his own mother. Maybe she's finally grown up, he thought, then shook his head, comprehending the strangeness of such a thought for an eleven-year-old boy to have of his mother.

Jimmy turned and descended the stairs. His mother, pleased and somewhat surprised by her boy's obedience, softened her tone.

"James, I'm not going to interrogate you about where you were all last night," she said.

"Okay," said Jimmy.

"I'm actually very proud of you for being able to handle yourself out there. I think this means you're all grown up," she said.

Jimmy stood there in silence, marveling at the strangeness of the conversation.

"Young man," she continued, "I have something to tell you that I didn't think you'd be ready to hear until you were mature enough."

Chloe Branhoover led her son from the foyer to the living room, where they sat down near the hearth.

"Do you remember the Christmas when you were five years old and we sat right here and you were opening presents, and one of the presents said 'To: Bernard, From: Santa.' "

"Yes," said Jimmy.

"And you thought Santa had made a mistake," said Chloe.

"Yes," said Jimmy, semi-laughing.

"It wasn't exactly a mistake, James," she said. "Bernard is a real boy. He is your older brother."

Jimmy was silent.

"You have an older brother, James. His name is Bernard. He is thirty-one years old now. He left for Las Vegas when he was eighteen, before you were born," she said.

"Way before I was born," said Jimmy, stoically.

"I'm sorry, James, I should have told you then, when you were five. And I shouldn't have taken you away from your friends at school. I'll take you back tomorrow and reenroll you," said Mrs. Branhoover.

"That's okay, Mom," said Jimmy. "I don't want to go back there anyway."

28. A Case of Mistaken Identity

H. Charles Branhoover experienced a curious (and perhaps ironic) side effect to his septuagenarian dementia: he began to notice and take an interest in things other than himself. He wandered the halls and rooms of his home during all hours of the days and nights, occasionally encountering his wife ("Hello, Milady," he would say) and his second son, whom he mistook for his first son.

"Bernard," he said to Jimmy, "we need to talk about your behavior. You can't be throwing rocks with angry letters attached through my office window. Now, I love you, son, so I'm not going to punish you. Instead I'm going to give you an opportunity. What do you know about Las Vegas?"

As luck would have it, Chloe's confession to Jimmy about his older brother had occurred the previous day, so Jimmy understood immediately that his elderly father thought he was speaking to Jimmy's mysterious older brother and didn't actually intend to send the eleven-year-old away to Las Vegas.

"You've mistaken me for Bernard," said Jimmy. "He doesn't live here anymore. I'm James, your second son."

H. Charles Branhoover examined the features of his second son's face for what seemed like an eternity to Jimmy. And then, finally convinced of the veracity of the boy's assertion, H. Charles Branhoover said, "And so you are. Delighted to meet you, James."

Father and son shook hands and went their separate ways.

29. My Name Is Vander Stevenson. I Am a Man of God.

As was customary and right, and as always, Mrs. Sunday arrived at the pulpit in her family's church and opened the service with her sermon, "The Life of a Hurricane."

Then Mr. Sunday joined his wife and proclaimed, "God is in the distant cosmos. This is true. Also true: You are the distant cosmos and God is in you. Hear the good news!"

The congregation might have thought good news was preceded by the scent of patchouli, because just as Mr. Sunday had uttered the words "good news," the man Kay Sunday had dubbed the Reverend Patchouli Goldwatch stood up and announced: "My name is Vander Stevenson. I am a man of God." Then he fired a precision strike of theological missiles at the Sundays, who simply lacked the moxie to respond in kind.

The man of God concluded by offering the congregation an alternative to what he called "far-out astrology."

"My church is literally across the road," he said, "and I promise my services will be light-years closer to your hearts and souls than the Sundays' well-intentioned but misguided lunacy."

Many in the congregation began to chuckle under their breaths. The Reverend Patchouli Goldwatch wiggled his leg when he heard their laughter.

30. Bon Voyage

Kay Sunday and the Innocents sniffed high-octane fumes and testified.

Kay: You know what today is?

Innocent #2: Tuesday?

Kay: That's right. Which means it was just two days ago when the Devil himself, the Reverend Patchouli Goldwatch, mustered enough nerve in his cowardly thin body to stand up in my parents' church and mock our faith.

Innocent #2: He's going straight to Hell!

Kay: Which means it was just yesterday when my parents sat me down on this very porch and informed me that they have been planning a mission to Cambodia and that they are going to finance it by selling our church and telescope. Can you guess who the buyer is?

Innocent #2: No!?

Kay: Yes. Vander Stevenson. Man of God. The Devil himself.

Innocent #2: We can't let this happen.

Kay: It's too late. The Sundays are moving to Cambodia.

Innocent #2: What about your house?

Kay: We rent it.

Innocent #2: How could they sell out so easily?

Kay: You know my parents. They see everything as a sign. Plus, they said Goldwatch made a generous offer.

Innocent #2: I'm not surprised. Innocent #1, don't you have anything to say about this?

Innocent #1: Bon voyage, Kay.

[Innocent #2 lunges at Innocent #1. The two boys fight feebly.]

Kay: Stop it, right now! Jimmy, go home. We don't want you here anymore.

Innocent #2: Yeah, get the fuck out of here.

Innocent #1: I've got better places to be anyway.

Jimmy picked up the gas can and hurled it off the porch, drenching the Sundays' lawn. He gave

Innocent #2 a final shove and walked off in the direction of the rows of destitute men.

31. Street Reflection

The Salvation Army thrift store was eight miles from the Sundays' front porch. This meant Jimmy had several hours of street reflection, which differs from the various forms of sedentary reflection in the same way that a stream differs from a pond.

Pond reflection tends toward the serene, with placid resolutions that grow stagnant and mossy if not acted upon. Street reflection leads to immediate, vigorous action, the consequences of which often become corrosive or destructive.

For eight miles Jimmy walked the streets of Pittsburgh, reflecting on the events of his recent past.

Those whom he had trusted, or perhaps more accurately, those whom he had relied upon in the years closest to his birth—his mom, his dad, and Kay—had each let him down in a uniquely monumental way.

He tried hard to understand how his mom could withhold from him the fact of his older brother for the first eleven years of his life. He considered the physical characteristics of every thirtyish male who passed by and wondered if his brother might be dead. This thought made him squirm with helplessness.

Then he considered the haplessness of his father when he mistook Jimmy for his possibly deceased older brother. His father: a spiritual wastrel festering in his own money and lust, in his trivial American success, for seventy years. That Jimmy was a product of these artificial ingredients was the second-most demoralizing aspect of his first eleven years.

Most demoralizing was the deterioration of his friendship with Kay Sunday. For all her otherworldly charm, Kay was maddeningly mercurial. Jimmy imagined her favorite shot in billiards would be the break, the colorful spheres scattering and bumping off the cushions and each other and occasionally dropping into the pockets by chance. This was the only plausible explanation for Kay's affection for Innocent #2. The colorful sphere that was Kay had randomly bumped around the pool table of Pittsburgh and dropped into a side pocket with the colorful sphere of Innocent #2.

For eight miles H. James Branhoover walked the streets of Pittsburgh reflecting on his parents, his brother, and Kay.

The strain on his mind produced an unusual thought: that the Salvation Army thrift store was more his home and his homeless acquaintances more his friends than were his actual home and so-called friends.

In the moving stream of his street reflection, Jimmy decided that he would spend an entire week with his three new friends, standing alongside the rows of destitute men and sorting out his religion in his notebook.

32. The Rising Sun

Jimmy arrived with the rising sun at the Salvation Army thrift store. He walked eagerly along the filthy row like a boy at an airport searching the faces for his long-lost brothers.

The men were mostly gathered in clusters, so it was difficult to distinguish one face from another. Then he noticed isolated at the far end of the row the wool blanket the honest man had given him on his previous visit. Next to the wool blanket lay the bruised, scraped, and bloodied body of the honest man and the green shards of Tanqueray and Rolling Rock bottles, the myriad facets of which glittered in the bright morning light.

Despite all the awful news that had recently befallen him, Jimmy reacted with the tranquility and patience of a triage nurse in coming to the aid of his friend. He carefully removed his notebook from his coat pocket and used it to sweep away the shards of glass.

Next, because he didn't know the honest man's name, he identified himself by the name the honest man had given him.

"Sir, it's Angel. Are you okay? I'm here to help you," said Jimmy.

"Angel? Is it really you?" asked the honest man, unable to open his eyes.

"Yes," said Jimmy. "Who did this to you? What happened?"

"I can't stop drinking," said the honest man. "Could you sit with me until this passes?"

"That's why I'm here," said Jimmy.

Jimmy sat down next to the honest man and rested his back against the thrift store wall. He opened his notebook, clicked open the ballpoint pen that served as a bookmark, jotted down a few lines, and promptly fell asleep.

By the time Jimmy woke, the sun was in the western sky. His face and lips were sunburned, and his sinuses ached from hours of incessant snoring.

The honest man was also awake now, sitting next to Jimmy like a bloodied watchdog. He had managed to remain conscious despite his injuries and hangover in order to watch over the sleeping Jimmy, who was also being watched by the inveterate grifter from one of the clusters of loitering men.

It took the inveterate grifter until dusk to concoct a scheme for separating Jimmy from his money. He approached the honest man and his angel, and addressed the honest man first.

"Rough night, eh?" said the inveterate grifter. "I'll withhold the embarrassing details."

"Unless I committed a crime, you know I'd prefer to be spared further humiliation," the honest man replied.

"You didn't do anything nefarious that I saw. Well, except what you did to yourself. It's a shame; it truly is. I know you're a good man. And I've already forgotten what you called me," said the inveterate grifter.

"Oh, dear," said the honest man. "You know I didn't mean it, whatever it was."

"Now that raises the age-old question going all the way back to Bible times: Do we believe the drunk in his sober remorse, or do we believe the drunk when he's drunk?"

The honest man grimaced and slumped against the thrift store wall.

The inveterate grifter then turned his attention toward Jimmy.

"What does the Bible have to say about drinking and drunks, young man?" he asked. "Have you written anything down in that notebook of yours that might be of use? Is there a miracle we have failed to acknowledge?"

Jimmy thought for a moment. Then he leafed through his notebook and read aloud: "Proverbs

23:20-21. 'Do not join those who drink too much wine or gorge themselves on meat, for drunkards and gluttons become poor, and drowsiness clothes them in rags.' And Proverbs 23:31-35. 'Do not gaze at wine when it is red, when it sparkles in the cup, when it goes down smoothly! In the end it bites like a snake and poisons like a viper. Your eyes will see strange sights and your mind imagine confusing things. You will be like one sleeping on the high seas, lying on top of the rigging. "They hit me," you will say, "but I'm not hurt! They beat me, but I don't feel it! When will I wake up so I can find another drink?" ' "

The honest man nodded and groaned.

"Oh, those Proverbs are as wise as they are pretty to hear," said the inveterate grifter. "And what does the Bible have to say about charity?"

While Jimmy scanned his mind for chapter and verse, the quiet man emerged from a cluster of men and joined Jimmy and the other two.

"What has the inveterate incompetent been saying to you, Freakshow?" asked the quiet man.

"I've been keeping an eye on him since he swooped down on you."

"He just asked me what the Bible says about charity," said Jimmy.

The quiet man made a sound like an air brake on a truck.

"No he didn't, Freakshow," said the quiet man. "What he asked you over many convoluted words and sentences was 'Can I have your money?'"

The honest man managed to smile through his battered face.

"Maybe he's starving but too proud to just come out and say it," said Jimmy, who reached into his pocket, pulled out five 20-dollar bills, and handed one of them to the inveterate grifter.

"Put those away, Freakshow," whispered the quiet man.

"He's right, Angel," said the honest man. "You mustn't do that around here."

But H. James Branhoover wasn't done handing out twenties. He handed one to the quiet man, who accepted it in spite of himself, and he slipped two in the honest man's shirt pocket, which left Jimmy with one twenty-dollar bill, which meant he wouldn't be able to stay for a week.

"I'll need this one for my ride home," said Jimmy, putting the money back into his pocket, rising from the Salvation Army thrift store wall, and walking off in search of a cab, utterly unaware of the force with which he had insulted these men.

33. Heavy Drapes

Chloe Branhoover had pulled back the heavy drapes from the living room window and watched the street all through the night before, when her son had walked eight miles along the streets of Pittsburgh.

When he didn't arrive home, she went upstairs and tried to find comfort in the televangelists, which meant she wanted to fall asleep.

But because the words of the televangelists are specifically fashioned to infiltrate the hearts of the vulnerable, Chloe Branhoover, like her son when he listened from his bedroom, remained rapt until morning.

She finally succumbed to sleep when the *Today* show came on and was still unconscious when Jimmy arrived home. She was dreaming about smear the queer when the sound of Jimmy's bedroom door clicking shut roused her. She spent several minutes thinking about how she would confront her son, but instead of entering his bedroom, she went downstairs and climbed into bed with her husband, who (unknown to her) had passed away about the time when Jimmy was giving away his father's money to the three homeless men.

34. Trust Fund Baby

Mrs. Chloe Branhoover stretched her arm across her husband's cold chest under the covers. Several minutes passed before she understood that he was gone.

First she thought about the heavy drapes. Then she thought about her son. Then, in the way that only a mature adult can do, she banished her own pain and went upstairs to tell her boy of this latest adverse truth.

Jimmy was writing in his notebook when his mother entered his bedroom. Once again she had that calm, kind, and loving expression that Jimmy was coming to dread as the inevitable harbinger of terrible news.

Chloe sat at the foot of her son's bed.

"What are you writing about?" she asked.

"I'm writing a letter to Kay," he said.

"Oh," she exclaimed, with both genuine and pleasant surprise that she wouldn't be forced to feign interest in his latest religious zealotry.

"Kay's a special girl," said Chloe, "but I wouldn't get too close to her. She's fickle."

Jimmy, who had rarely done so before, even as an infant, began to sob. His mother, who had rarely done so before, embraced him with genuine vigor, as if she had just been told for the first time that this boy was her son.

Jimmy explained to her about the high-octane sessions on Kay's porch and how Kay had changed since the better days of Mrs. Germany and the Carden School. All Mrs. Branhoover could do was nod with compassion and comprehension, which was all Jimmy needed to fortify himself for the latest bad news he knew his mother was preparing to impart to him.

"What happened, Mom?" asked Jimmy.

"I'm just going to tell you everything, okay?" said Chloe.

Jimmy nodded.

"Your father is dead, Jimmy. He passed last night in his sleep."

Jimmy nodded again.

"We are a wealthy family," she said.

Jimmy rolled his eyes. "I know that, Mom. I'm not two," he said warmly.

"Well, what I mean to convey is that your father was frugal with our money, but that's going to change now, Jimmy."

"Okay," he said.

"He set up a trust for you that I now have control over until you turn eighteen. I want you to take responsibility for your own decisions, so whenever you need money, just let me know and I'll get it for you, no questions asked," she said.

"Really? How much money is in the trust?"

"I'm not sure of the exact amount, but it's in the neighborhood of ten million dollars," Chloe said.

H. James Branhoover, the Branhoovers' second son, let out a staccato laugh of shocked disbelief.

"Ten million?" he repeated.

Chloe Branhoover laughed brightly. "You're a millionaire," she said.

"Any more bad news?" asked Jimmy.

"There is one more thing," she said. "Kristina Sunday called yesterday. She said that she and her husband sold their church to a more persuasive man of God."

"You mean the Devil?" said Jimmy, restraining a grin.

Mrs. Branhoover did her best to maintain a neutral expression.

"She said the Sundays are moving to Cambodia."

Jimmy shrugged with unconvincing nonchalance.

"Anything else?"

PART VI

35. Bright Red Swastika

Vander Stevenson, aka the Reverend Patchouli Goldwatch, took immediate steps to obliterate the eccentric art on the Sundays' former church.

Initially remaining true to his promise of offering an alternative to the Sundays' "far-out astrology," Stevenson painted the exterior of the structure Southern Baptist white, and he put the telescope in storage.

Attendance began to drop almost immediately. The congregation was having a difficult time reconciling Southern Baptist white with the man who painted a yin/yang symbol on a wigwam.

Goldwatch understood that he needed to divert the negative attention away from him and put it back on the Sundays, as he had done so successfully before.

He thought about all the ways he could defame the Sundays. There were so many. Then he said, "Kristov, Kristina, Kay. KKK."

He went to his new church late on Saturday evening and worked all through the night so that come Sunday morning the congregation would arrive to see a bright red swastika painted on the side of the building.

36. Proper Swastika

For the first time in the history of the church, there was an overflow line (stretching several yards out the door) to attend a Sunday service. Goldwatch remained inside until he could hear the line begin to hum like a mob. Then he rose in the pulpit and called for the entire congregation to gather outside.

Standing in front of his new creation, Goldwatch explained the long history and true spiritual significance of the swastika prior to the Nazis' misappropriation of it.

He explained how the swastika symbolizes good luck, protection, circular movement and rebirth, and how his swastika's arms faced left and not right like the Nazis'.

Then he turned his attention to the Sundays. He announced with authority the initials of their names—KKK—and how their quirky brand of religion, seemingly benign, was actually deliberately designed to distract true Christians from the teachings and message of Christ.

Half of the congregation—the credulous half—applauded the Reverend and began to move toward the entrance. The other half of the congregation—the skeptics and the amateur astronomers—grumbled and began to disperse, including Innocent #2, who shouted to anyone with ears within a square mile of the church: "Charlatan!"

37. Reconciliation of the Innocents

In the early days of the high-octane sessions on Kay Sunday's porch, Jimmy and Innocent #2 had exchanged phone numbers under the pretense of becoming friends and the tacit understanding—which was also plain to Kay, though the boys didn't acknowledge it—that neither boy had any intention whatsoever of calling the other.

All three children were students at the Carden School, with the established dynamic of Kay and Jimmy as best friends and Innocent #2 as a willing sidekick, though shorter and not as handsome as Jimmy, who had the good fortune of inheriting his father's looks.

Jimmy was certainly surprised when Innocent #2 called him to apologize for putting him on the spot at Kay Sunday's, as well as to confide in him about his feelings for her and about Goldwatch defaming the Sundays with his swastika stunt.

Jimmy was equally surprised by his own reaction to the call. He couldn't abide the words coming out of his mouth:

"Apology accepted," he said, regarding their confrontation on Kay's porch.

"Let's come up with a plan to get Goldwatch out of the Sundays' church," he said, shocked to hear himself suggest that they work together.

But worst of all: "Kay has feelings for you, too. I think you would make a good couple."

Mercifully, Jimmy eventually found the courage to hang up, but not before he invited Innocent #2 over to discuss the Goldwatch situation.

After he hung up, he opened his notebook to a blank page and stared at it until his shame had subsided enough for him to reflect on what motivated him to say such deplorable things.

Ultimately, he concluded that his responses were not cowardly but perfectly brave, and probably the surest way to win Kay back. Remaining magnanimous toward Innocent #2 clearly seemed to be Jimmy's best option under the circumstances. He would prove to Kay once and for all that he was not jealous of Innocent #2 and was, in fact, more desirable than his adversary. Why shouldn't he be magnanimous? Compared to Innocent #2, he was smarter, taller, better-looking, had known Kay longer and was her best friend, and would take the initiative in getting the Sundays' church back from Goldwatch.

He was also much wealthier than Innocent #2, though he didn't include this item in his mental list.

38. No Octane

Innocent #1 and Innocent #2, sans Kay Sunday, met on the Sundays' former porch to plot the overthrow of Vander Stevenson, aka the Reverend Patchouli Goldwatch.

Jimmy: I saw the swastika on the Sundays' church. I can't believe there wasn't a riot.

Innocent #2: He attracted a crowd and then he blamed the swastika on the Sundays' first names. He connected them with the Ku Klux Klan and said that his "correct" swastika would purify the building.

Jimmy: And the people believed him?

Innocent #2: It didn't matter. Don't you see? The people weren't thinking about Goldwatch anymore. They were thinking about the Sundays and the KKK.

Jimmy: Hey, man, I get it. Don't talk to me like that.

Innocent #2: Like what?

Jimmy: Look, you little punk, I'm Kay's best friend. I'm the one who's going to get their church back for them. Not you.

Innocent #2: You don't get it. Kay doesn't like you the way she likes me, even if you do buy her church back from Goldwatch.

Jimmy: What do you mean, "buy" it?

Innocent #2: I'm sorry, Jimmy, I think you mean well, but you're deluded. You're totally sheltered and your parents are completely messed up. Kay and I feel sorry for you. I mean, you don't even go to school anymore.

Jimmy: You have no idea who I am, where I've been, what I've done, or who I've helped. You're just the short little sidekick who sniffs gasoline fumes with her and says something funny every now and then. That's the only reason Kay likes you. There's no threat of anything real, and that appeals to her because she's shallow.

Innocent #2: Then why do you like her so much?

Jimmy either had no answer to this question or didn't have the energy to explain it. He picked up his pen and notebook, and walked off the porch in the direction of the rows of destitute men.

39. Ten Thousand Dollars

H. James Branhoover was barely off the Sundays' former property when he determined there was no way he was going to suffer another eight-mile trudge through the less desirable neighborhoods of Pittsburgh. He found a convenience store and phoned his mother.

"I need ten thousand dollars to take down to skid row," he said.

"Okay, James," she said, already regretting her promise to him. "I'll phone the bank now."

"Thanks, Mom," said Jimmy, and he hung up the phone.

Jimmy took a cab to the bank, which presented only one obstacle to his attainment of ten thousand dollars: another quick call to his mother so that she could identify her son's voice. And that was that. The teller counted out ninety 100 dollar bills and fifty 20s, zipped them up neatly in a relatively easy-to-carry pouch, and handed it to the twelve-year-old boy across the counter.

Jimmy felt nauseated when he climbed back into the cab and headed off to see his three friends at the Salvation Army thrift store.

In the backseat of the cab, he sat holding his pouch of money and ruminating on his latest confrontation with Innocent #2.

He couldn't understand why he couldn't control his temper and remain magnanimous, even under the circumstances.

He couldn't understand why he didn't sock the little punk in the nose.

"Kay and I feel sorry for you." What a joke. They're the ones who sniff gasoline fumes, not me, he thought.

Mercifully, this inner debate concluded when the cab pulled up at the Salvation Army thrift store and Jimmy saw the honest man waiting for him with clear eyes and clean clothes.

"Hello, young man," said the honest man when Jimmy stepped out of the cab.

Jimmy instinctively reached out his right hand, which the honest man instinctively grabbed and shook, the entire apparatus of the transaction slightly embarrassing the two of them.

"What happened?" asked Jimmy. "I'm sorry, it's just that you look completely different. I mean, you look better."

"I got religion," said the honest man. "I'm going to AA meetings and am looking into the jobs program over at Goodwill."

"Why? What changed?" asked Jimmy.

"Now don't let this go to your head, but it was you. Your commitment to God and your notebook and 'how can you fail to acknowledge the miracle' and all that," said the honest man. "Hey, listen, I don't believe I know your name, unless your name is Angel," he said, laughing.

"Haley James Branhoover," said Jimmy, surprised to hear himself announce his full name and to hear the authoritative tone of his voice. "But I go by Jimmy or James," he continued.

"It's a pleasure to meet you, James," said the honest man. "My name is Charles Larson." The two of them were unable to resist the urge to shake hands again.

"Charles was my father's name," said Jimmy. "He passed away recently."

"I'm sorry to hear that, Angel," said Charles Larson.

"Thanks," said Jimmy, and quickly changed the subject. "I brought something for you and your friends," he said, unzipping the pouch and showing the honest man the ten thousand dollars.

"Put that away!" said Charles. "You mustn't do that. You're going to get yourself robbed and killed. And those two aren't my friends. Come to think of it, they're not your friends either. They wanted to hurt you when you shoved your money in their faces the last time. You mustn't ever do that again, James."

"Then I want you to have all of it," said Jimmy. "Get yourself an apartment and some clothes for your new job. Charles—my dad—was loaded. I've got millions more where this came from. I want you to take this."

The honest man took the pouch, shoved it down the front of his pants, and then covered it up with his untucked shirt.

"Thank you, Angel," said Charles Larson, clean and sober and floating on a pink cloud, all because he acknowledged the miracle that Haley James Branhoover brought to the rows of destitute men.

40. Pink Cloud, Red Paint

H. James Branhoover was so overwhelmed by what he had just done—no one, not Innocent #2 or Kay Sunday, his dead father, or even the quiet man or the inveterate grifter, could deny that he had saved a man's life—that he wept in the cab on the way home.

Surely this was what the late-night televangelists were trying to tell him from the room across the hall while his mother tried desperately to sleep.

Surely Jimmy had been entrusted with the boon of his father's inheritance because he had the God-given desire to change people's lives. The money was simply an enabling tool. How could he fail to acknowledge the miracle?

He thought gently about his father—how God had designed him to be a ruthless, self-absorbed, philandering banker so that his fortune could be passed down to his God-fearing son, who would put the money to good use.

If Jimmy and his wisdom and his money could restore Charles Larson—a hopeless skid row alcoholic—to sanity, then what else could Jimmy do and who else could he save?

He opened his notebook to a blank page, stared at it for less than a minute, closed it, and told the cab driver to wait for him as the cab pulled into the Branhoovers' driveway.

Jimmy ran into the garage, grabbed a can of red spray paint, and then jumped back into the cab while his mother watched from the living room window under the weight of the drapes.

The next stop for the cab was the Sundays' former church, where Jimmy casually and conspicuously strolled up to Goldwatch's correct swastika, spray-painted over it, and then next to it painted a bright red 666 and the following prayer:

Lord Satan, make me an instrument of Thy chaos. Where there is hatred, let me be called among the haters; where there is injury, let

my wrath be the cause; where there is doubt,
let me be the spreader of lies; where there is
despair, let me extinguish the faltering flame;
where there is darkness, let my sullenness be
the cause; where there is sadness, let my mirth
twist and tear like a dagger. O Divine
Master, grant that I may not so much seek to
console as to be consoled, to understand as to
be understood, to love as to be loved. For it is
in receiving that we truly give, in being
pardoned for our transgressions that justice is
truly served, and in dying that we are truly
dead.

—*Vander Stevenson, Antichrist*

Jimmy stepped back and admired his work for a moment, then he turned and tossed the spray can as far as he could and began walking back toward the cab, which was no longer there, in its place a police car, and instead of a cab driver, two police officers.

"Is that your artwork on that church?" asked the first officer.

"I don't know what you're talking about," said Jimmy.

The second officer then grabbed Jimmy's hands and turned them palms up.

Jimmy grinned. "Looks like I've been caught red-handed," he said.

41. Smug Jimmy

H. James Branhoover sat in the police station with a smug expression while the officers tried to scare him with high-end cost estimates for the property damage and the damage his stunt would do to his reputation in the community.

To the latter Jimmy reminded them that he was a minor, so his identity was off-limits; to the former he said nothing, confident in his new knowledge that his money could absolve him of the consequences of his antics.

Eventually the officers lost interest in the young perp and let him make his phone call. When Jimmy told his mother where he was and what he had done, she began to cry.

Jimmy couldn't believe it. What is going on with her? he thought.

When Jimmy and Chloe arrived home after she picked him up at the station, Chloe hugged Jimmy and said, "I hope you don't turn out like your brother, though I could hardly blame you if you did."

42. Top Jimmy

First thing the following morning was the first time H. James Branhoover had been the one to retrieve the newspaper from the front porch of his home.

And there it was. The headline on page one of the local section of the *Pittsburgh Post-Gazette* read "Precocious Minor Defaces Swastika Church with Anti-Simple Prayer."

Jimmy read the article from beginning to end half a dozen times before he showed it to his mom. Chloe Branhoover read the headline aloud to her son, and though she tried to muster enthusiasm for the phrase "Precocious Minor," her worried expression belied her obsession with the notion that her second boy was going to turn out like her first boy.

"I'm proud of you, James," she said. "You're a creative and intelligent young man. But what you did was a crime. Do you understand that? What you did harmed someone."

"What I did was expose the devil that swindled the Sundays and took their church," said Jimmy.

Mrs. Branhoover took a moment of thoughtful silence. "I know how much you like Kay Sunday, but she's not the one for you, James," she said. "You could pull off a hundred more of these quixotic triumphs, but it won't make a difference where Kay is concerned. She's made up her mind about you and that will never change."

"With all due respect, Mom, I find it difficult to take relationship advice from you," said Jimmy. "And besides, that's not why I painted the church."

"Okay, James," she said, and walked into the living room to resume her post at the window.

* * * * *

Jimmy couldn't contain his excitement. He needed to talk to someone who would truly appreciate what he had done. He picked up the phone and dialed Innocent #2.

"Brilliant, Jimmy. Absolutely inspired," said Innocent #2, who had already read the article even more times than Jimmy had. "What are the cops going to do to you?"

"I don't know," said Jimmy. "Some kind of restitution, I'm sure. But who cares, right? I can pay it however much it is," he said, laughing.

"Trust fund baby!" exclaimed Innocent #2. "Send the devil Goldwatch running! Hey, I'm going to write Kay and tell her the good news."

The fireflies in Jimmy's head promptly transformed into a lead weight, which dropped into the pit of his stomach.

"Definitely," said Jimmy, trying to revive the good insects now moldering in his abdomen. "Hey, I've got to go. My mom's calling me," said Jimmy.

"Cool," said Innocent #2. "I'll write the letter to Kay and drop it in the mail first thing tomorrow."

Jimmy hung up the phone, slammed the newspaper against the wall, and called a cab to take him to find Charles Larson.

43. Charles Larson

"Skid row?" asked the cab driver when Jimmy slid into the back of the cab. He looked into the rearview mirror and examined the cabby's eyes, which were mirthful and eager to make sport of him.

Jimmy forced a neutral expression and extinguished the light in his eyes.

"Goodwill," he said. Not another word was spoken between the two of them.

At Goodwill, Jimmy walked directly to the reception desk and asked for Charles Larson.

"Are you his son?" asked the receptionist.

"No, just a friend," said Jimmy, trying to conceal his shock.

"He's not scheduled today, but you can try tomorrow. He's due in at ten o'clock," she said.

"Can you call him and tell him James is here to see him?" asked Jimmy.

The receptionist shrugged. "Sure," she said, and dialed the number.

"Mr. Larson?" she said. "It's Darla at Goodwill. There's a boy called James here to visit you . . . I don't know, let me ask him."

"James, would you mind seeing Mr. Larson at his apartment?"

"Not at all," said Jimmy.

The excitement in his voice startled Darla, who gave Jimmy Mr. Larson's address, which was less than a mile away.

"James!" exclaimed Charles Larson, opening the door before Jimmy could even knock.

The two gentlemen shook hands for the third time, and Charles Larson took Jimmy on a thorough, five-minute tour of his sparsely furnished, yet tidy, studio apartment.

Jimmy sat down on Larson's Murphy bed, so overwhelmed by the positive outcome of his charity that he laughed and wept simultaneously.

Charles Larson sat next to Jimmy and stroked his leg. "It's all because of you, Angel," he said.

Jimmy leapt to his feet. "What the hell are you doing?!" he exclaimed.

"Nothing, Angel," said Charles Larson. "I'm just a tactile person when I'm happy."

Jimmy took a moment to calm himself. "Okay," he said. "It's just . . . can you please stop calling me Angel?"

"Of course, James. You're a decent young man and your name is James. I respect you and I apologize," said Charles Larson. "Anyway, I'm doing well. I am still sober since we last spoke and my plan is to do janitorial work to put myself through school. My goal is to become a nurse, James," he said.

"That's great," said Jimmy, still deflated by what he considered a violation of his person. "Well, I'd better get going. I'm sure my mom's looking out the window wondering where I am," he said, trying to mask his fear with a feeble smile.

"Of course, of course," said Charles Larson. "You mustn't worry your mother."

The two gentlemen shook hands again and Jimmy walked out the door and back to Goodwill, where he called a cab and went directly home, his eyes downcast and wide, and his pride shaken.

44. Every Maternal Nerve

Chloe Branhoover was so pleased to see the cab arrive in her driveway on the same day as its departure that she had to catch her breath before her son walked in the door.

H. James Branhoover embraced his mother tightly and then explained how his work on skid row was complete.

Every maternal nerve in Chloe's body comprehended that something had happened to her boy down there, but every maternal instinct told her now was not the time to press him on it.

"I'm so glad you accomplished your goal, Jimmy, but I'm even happier that I don't have to worry about you getting hurt down there," she said, with equal parts nervousness and relief in her voice.

"I'm sorry, Mom," said Jimmy. "I promise I won't go down there anymore."

"Thank you, James," she said. "Oh, your friend, um, Innocent #2 called. He wants you to call him back about the Reverend Patchouli Goldwatch. Does that make sense?"

Jimmy laughed. "Believe it or not, it does," he said and walked upstairs to his bedroom, where he fell asleep within minutes.

45. It Can't Be That Dire

Jimmy spent the first several hours of the following morning preparing his nerves and his patience for the phone call, promising himself that he wouldn't get angry. He was so intensely focused on his mock conversations with Innocent #2 that he didn't hear the phone ring.

"James," said his mother from downstairs, "um, Innocent #2 is on the phone for you."

Jimmy was immediately annoyed, but he forced himself to mind his emotions before he picked up the receiver.

"Hello?" said H. James Branhoover.

"Jimmy, hey!" exclaimed Innocent #2. "You'll never guess who I just talked to."

"I don't know . . . Kay," he said flatly.

"No, no," he said. "Goldwatch! You're not even going to believe me, but he says he might be willing to give the Sundays their church back."

"Are you serious?" said Jimmy. "Did you threaten to kill him or something?"

Both boys laughed.

"Nah, nothing like that, but I'll store the thought away for later," said Innocent #2.

"What did you say?" asked Jimmy.

"I told him you were willing to buy him out," said Innocent #2. "I told him you are loaded."

Jimmy exploded. "You little punk!" he screamed, and then he remembered his precall pep talk, set the receiver down, and walked away for a moment.

When he picked up the phone again, he heard a dial tone.

Mrs. Branhoover tried to comfort her second son. "Are you okay, sweetheart?"

"I'm fine, Mom," said Jimmy, again surprised and pleased by her compassion.

"Does this have something to do with Kay Sunday?" she asked. "I understand how painful this must be, James, but I promise that someday you'll meet a girl who won't make you feel so angry and confused."

"It's not about Kay," said Jimmy. "It's about what I'm willing to pay for right over wrong."

"It can't be that dire, sweetheart, you're just a boy," she said.

46. Strong First Impression, but Not a Lasting One

Jimmy stayed awake into the early hours of the morning in an attempt to honestly appraise his motives should he decide, against all better instinct, to meet with Goldwatch to buy back the Sundays' church.

Was it as simple as his mom had insisted? That he was trying to impress Kay? Or was it truly as dire a matter as right versus wrong, or even good versus evil?

Jimmy stared at a blank page in his notebook considering these questions, ultimately concluding that impressing Kay Sunday would be nothing more than a collateral reward for doing what was right, and that, like his work with the rows of destitute men, his true motives were righteousness and redemption. How could he fail to acknowledge the miracle of Charles Larson? If his mom knew about Charles Larson, surely she would agree that there was more at stake than impressing a girl.

That settled it. H. James Branhoover was going to buy back the Sundays' church, and his motive for doing so was, if not pure, at least right enough.

* * * * *

Jimmy called Innocent #2 the moment he awoke the next day.

"I thought about it all last night, and I think buying the church back from Goldwatch is the right thing to do," he said.

"I think so, too," said Innocent #2.

"But when I meet with him, I don't want you to be there," said Jimmy, unconcerned by his bluntness.

"I understand," said Innocent #2, who then gave Goldwatch's phone number to Jimmy and hung up without saying goodbye.

* * * * *

Jimmy put the receiver in its holder and immediately picked it up again before he could think about chickening out. He dialed Goldwatch's number.

"Vander Stevenson," said the voice on the other end, which for a split second caused Jimmy to think he had dialed the wrong number.

"Hello?" said Goldwatch.

"Sir," said Jimmy, "my name is Haley James Branhoover. I'm the one who . . ."

Goldwatch let out a screwball laugh that put Jimmy at ease.

"You're the clever boy who painted the anti-Simple Prayer on the side of my church," said Goldwatch.

"Sorry about that," said Jimmy.

"Don't be sorry, Haley. I'm not sorry you did it. In fact, I'm glad you did it, and now let me tell you why," said Goldwatch.

"You can call me James," said Jimmy.

"And you can call me Vander . . . or Mr. Stevenson, if you think it strange to call an adult by his first name," said Goldwatch.

"Mr. Stevenson it is," said Jimmy.

"That's fine, James," said Goldwatch. "James," he said, "I'm a man who makes a strong first impression but doesn't leave a lasting one. That's why I'm glad you did what you did and am insisting that any charges or restitution be dropped. Now hear me out, James. You see, I'm not a man of God, necessarily. I'm more of a businessman. And from what Innocent #2 tells me—and forgive me for saying so, but that boy is contemptible—you have the means to purchase the church back for the Sundays, and I would get a tidy profit in return," said Goldwatch.

"That sounds about right," said Jimmy, pleased to hear that charges would likely be dropped and that Stevenson held the same low opinion of Innocent #2 that he did. "And what exactly do you mean you make a strong first impression but don't leave a lasting one?"

"As early as I can remember, people have been drawn to me and my screwball stunts. It's the damnedest thing, James," said Goldwatch. "Now hear me out. Take the swastika stunt, for example. It doesn't get more screwball than that, but people bought it, James, and I'll admit I am addicted to the power of my own charisma, how it gets me what I want with such little resistance. But, and it's the damnedest thing, the same people I can charm so quickly are the same people who turn on me equally quick. I like to get in and out as fast as possible, and that's why I am willing to accept any reasonable offer you make for the purchase of the property."

"Well, okay then," said Jimmy. "I think $200,000 over what you paid for the property is reasonable. Do you agree?"

"I think that is beyond reasonable, James. In fact, I think it is downright generous. I accept your offer," said Stevenson.

"Great," said Jimmy. "That wasn't so bad at all."

"Not bad at all. Pleasant even," said Stevenson.

"What next? I'll call Innocent #2 with the good news, and he can write the Sundays to let them know I'm giving them the money to buy back their church," said Jimmy.

"Oh, they are going to be thrilled," said Stevenson. "Until next time."

"Until then," said Jimmy.

47. A Telegram

Innocent #2 sent a telegram to the Sundays in Cambodia, which read as follows:

DEAR KRISTOV, KRISTINA, AND KAY: UNDER MY DIRECTION, JIMMY BRANHOOVER PAINTED ANTI-SIMPLE PRAYER ON GOLDWATCH'S CHURCH. GOLDWATCH LOST SUPPORT OF CONGREGATION AND AGREED TO SELL CHURCH BACK TO YOU. JIMMY BRANHOOVER WILL GIFT YOU THE FUNDS FOR THE REPURCHASE.
YOURS, INNOCENT #2

Kris and Kris were shocked and thrilled by the news. The people of Cambodia had been kind, if unreceptive, to the Sundays' brand of religion, though they enjoyed Mrs. Sunday's hurricane sermon, which she called "The Life of a Typhoon."

Kay, however, was sullen, which her parents found incomprehensible. Mrs. Sunday pleaded with her daughter. "But you hate it here, Kay," she said. "Your father and I are getting our church back from the preacher you hated so much, and you get to go home to your boyfriend and see your old friend Jimmy, too. What an unbelievably generous thing for Jimmy to do. He is turning into a remarkable young man."

"The only thing remarkable about Jimmy is his money, and it's not even his, really, it's his rotten old man's," said Kay. "Did you read the telegram? This wasn't even his idea, it was my boyfriend's. Jimmy thinks he can buy me, but he's just a friend, and he's not even that anymore."

"Honestly, Kay!" exclaimed Mrs. Sunday. "Such hateful things to say about Jimmy Branhoover. You should be grateful, and nothing else, for what he has done. If you want to know the truth, James is a finer young man than your boyfriend."

"H. James Branhoover is a dope, Mom," said Kay Sunday, who then silenced her furious mother with a hug and the long, deep stare of her otherworldly eyes.

PART VII

48. Two Letters

The Sundays needed approximately one month to wind up and dissolve their operation in Cambodia, during which time Kay sent Jimmy the following letter:

Dear Jimmy:

I'm going to come straight to the point: You can't buy me. Your money means nothing. Innocent #2 is my boyfriend, and I know this whole thing was his idea. You wouldn't have had the guts to do any of this on your own. You were mostly silent concerning Goldwatch during the high-octane sessions, and you barely took part in the ritual of the fumes.

–Kay

And Jimmy sent the following reply:

Dear Kay:

You know damned well it wasn't his idea to paint the anti-Simple Prayer on your church. He doesn't even know who St. Francis of Assisi is. I'm giving your parents the money to get their church back and am sending the Devil packing. I have no desire to "buy" you or otherwise take anything from you, so you might as well start being nice. Also, I'd like to resume the high-octane sessions when you return. I can promise you, I won't be mostly silent.

Sincerely,

Jimmy

49. Clever and Full of Grace

Kay Sunday and the Innocents sniffed high-octane fumes and testified.

Kay: Now I'm just going to come right out and say it. Jimmy Branhoover, you barely pass that gas can under your nose, let alone inhale as much as we do.

Jimmy: You can't be serious. We're sitting here on your brand-new porch in your fancy new home, you never have to go back to Cambodia for as long as you live, your parents got their church back, you got your boyfriend back, the Reverend Patchouli Goldwatch—the Devil himself—is gone for good, and all you can do is give me grief for not wanting to give myself brain damage just for the sake of some idiotic ritual.

Kay: Look who's the rooster man now, all proud of that stupid anti-prayer he got lucky and painted, and his rotten old man's money that he used to buy my family.

Jimmy: You know you're just talking now, Kay. You know that's not true. How could someone so clever and full of grace be so shallow?

Kay: Well, now, that's got to be the most interesting thing you've ever said. But it's too little, too late. You're nothing but a trust fund baby, H. James Branhoover. No one will ever respect you. Your opinion doesn't count.

Not another word was spoken. Jimmy picked up his notebook and quietly left the property, while Kay buried her face in her hands and sobbed. Innocent #2 sat staring at the ground, the handle of the gas can dangling from his index finger.

50. Aftermath

Jimmy Branhoover spent the first month after his falling-out with Kay Sunday in isolation in his room, reading his Bible and making entries in his notebook.

He noticed in his time of trouble that he was less and less interested in the Book of Revelation and more interested in the Psalms, Gospels, Ecclesiastes, and Epistles.

He used the Bible as a sort of Magic Eight Ball. He would ask it questions, open the Book, and then turn the pages until he found the answers he needed. He was especially interested in passages that his eyes tried to skip over because they made him uncomfortable. For example, "But love your enemies, and do good, and lend, expecting nothing back," and "Again I tell you, it is easier for a camel to go through the eye of a needle than for a rich man to enter the kingdom of God."

These verses made him squirm over his never-ending inability to reconcile his true motive for giving the Sundays the money to buy back their church. To make matters worse, from time to time he could hear his mother downstairs on the telephone talking to Kristina Sunday. They were becoming close friends. Jimmy couldn't believe how insensitive this was. If Jimmy were the father and Chloe were his daughter who had just suffered a falling-out with an acquaintance's son, there is no way he would be on the phone with the son's parent trying to become friends.

When Jimmy confronted her on this, Mrs. Branhoover said it wasn't what Jimmy was thinking at all. In fact, she said "Mrs. Sunday advocates on your behalf. She reminds Kay what a remarkable young man you are and tells her you would be better for her than Innocent #2." To which Jimmy grinned sarcastically and responded, "I'm sure that's really helping my cause."

"I remind Mrs. Sunday that Kay isn't the right girl for you," Chloe said.

The more Jimmy heard his mom say these words, the better, the lighter, he began to feel.

He started to think about the future. He wondered about Charles Larson.

51. A Scrubs-Clad Woman

Despite all the adverse truths in his first dozen years—his mom being an on-again-off-again prostitute; the death of his well-to-do and good-for-nothing father; his hitherto unknown and now absent older brother; his withdrawal from the Carden School; his confrontations with the quiet man, the inveterate grifter, and Vander Stevenson aka the Reverend Patchouli Goldwatch; his being arrested for spray-painting a church; and his falling-out with Kay Sunday—H. James

Branhoover was feeling pretty good about the way things were going.

I remind Mrs. Sunday that Kay isn't the right girl for you, Jimmy repeated in his mind. Chloe Branhoover had stuck up for her son and subtly implied to Mrs. Sunday that her daughter wasn't good enough for him. The otherworldly Kay, for all her grace and charm and wit, was ultimately a shallow girl, while Jimmy, a sheltered, mostly silent, undereducated trust fund baby, was ultimately a serious young man, learned in Bible verses and had led a hapless alcoholic away from skid row and into sobriety, possibly even into nursing school.

Jimmy began to fixate less on Kay Sunday and more on Charles Larson.

Still concerned about the thigh-stroking incident, Jimmy spent the first months of his fixation monitoring Charles Larson from the safety of taxi cabs. He would pass by Larson's apartment at different times on different days of the week.

Jimmy didn't always see Larson on these drive-bys, but when he did, Larson always appeared well-dressed (though in secondhand clothes) and sober, and always alone.

Jimmy made detailed entries in his notebook each time there was a sighting.

After a year went by, Jimmy noted a change in Larson's dress. He now wore scrubs as often as he did street clothes. And then something even more remarkable: every Tuesday and Thursday, Charles Larson would arrive home at noon in a car driven by a scrubs-clad woman. They would disappear behind Larson's apartment door for an hour and then they would reappear—always smiling and sometimes laughing—and drive off in the woman's car.

This was the evidence Jimmy was waiting for. He was no longer concerned about the thigh-stroking incident. He made entries in his notebook concerning the optimal time to reintroduce himself to the honest man and to introduce himself for the first time to the honest man's girlfriend.

52. Fifteenth Birthday

Chloe Branhoover had made good on her promise to allow her second son to make his own decisions with little or no maternal interference. This even included his birthdays.

On all of Jimmy's birthdays since the death of his father, Mrs. Branhoover would purchase a card and a modest gift—usually a new pen or notebook and the most luminous writings on religion she could find—and then she would give Jimmy his gift and kindly ask him his plans for the day.

On his fifteenth birthday, as on his recent birthdays, Jimmy graciously thanked his mother for pen/notebook/luminous religious work; but unlike the past few birthdays, he then informed her that he was going to drop in on an old friend for lunch.

"Not Kay Sunday?" said Mrs. Branhoover.

"No, Mom, not Kay. Someone you don't know, but I may introduce you to him someday. He's just an old friend."

"An old friend?" said Mrs. Branhoover. "You're only fifteen, James. You're too young to have an old friend that I don't know about. Is he from school?"

"No, he's not from school, but please don't worry. You'll meet him soon, I promise," said Jimmy, who picked up the telephone and called a cab.

* * * * *

The woman's car was already parked outside of Larson's apartment when Jimmy arrived via cab. He hastily paid the cab driver and jogged up to Larson's door.

"James!" exclaimed Larson, "so good to see you. I was wondering when you were going to visit again. All those cab rides must be getting expensive." He winked at Jimmy.

Jimmy blushed. "Well, I'm sure they weren't *all* me," he said. "Only four out of every five or so."

"I completely understand," said Larson. "I had to regain your trust. Please, come in. We're about to sit down for lunch."

The honest man escorted Jimmy to the kitchen table, making sure not to touch him in any way.

"James, I'd like to introduce you to my good friend and fellow nurse, Betsy Sullivan."

"Nice to meet you, Betsy Sullivan. My name is Haley James Branhoover," said Jimmy, surprised by the regal tone of his voice.

"Branhoover?" blurted Betsy. "I dated your brother in high school. Bernard or . . . Bernrd, whatever his name is. Ha! He used to call me 'fussy wet salami.' We were in love. How is he doing, James?"

The color exited Jimmy's face, and he grabbed the back of a kitchen chair.

"Um, I've never met my brother," said Jimmy, meekly.

"Well then, it looks like we've got something to talk about," said Betsy, trying to conceal any indication of shock or pity.

"You never told me you had a brother, James," said Charles Larson.

"I didn't even know about him until a couple of years ago," said Jimmy.

"I'm sorry, Angel," said Charles Larson.

"Let me tell you about Bernrd Red!" Betsy Sullivan interjected, exhibiting clear hostility toward soft emotions outside of the hospital setting.

"Bernrd Red? You must be mistaken. My brother's name is Bernard Branhoover."

"Who knows what he's calling himself these days. Could be anything," said Betsy. "Ha! When we were an item, he went by Bernrd Red. He deliberately removed the 'a' from 'Bernard' to irritate the teachers. And it worked! He was clever that way. He irritated me, too, at first. I socked him in the forehead at recess way back in elementary school. He hit me back, the bastard. That's how we were introduced. We were real troublemakers, but we were creative about it. Not like kids today."

"How old are you?" asked Jimmy.

"It's not polite to ask a woman her age," said Charles Larson.

"Thirty-five," said Betsy.

"Same age as my brother," said Jimmy.

"Yeah, sure," said Betsy. "And how old are you, young man?"

"Today is my fifteenth birthday," said Jimmy.

"Happy birthday, Angel!" shouted the honest man.

"Thanks," said Jimmy, thinking for a moment that in some better, alternate universe Charles Larson and Betsy Sullivan were his parents.

53. Harmonious Enough

The first months of Kay Sunday's post-Jimmy Branhoover years were harmonious enough. Her parents had resumed their rightful role as spiritual consultants and amateur astronomers, their spacey church with its telescope having been returned to them. She continued to charm and excel at the Carden School. And she and Innocent #2 were free at last to pursue to the fullest extent the triumph of the high-octane sessions—their relationship—without the perceived need to conceal it for the sake of Jimmy's feelings.

But for Kay "harmonious enough" was precisely the problem. She began to miss Jimmy, or, perhaps more accurately, she began to miss the thrill of the tension between Jimmy and Innocent #2, or, perhaps most accurately, she couldn't stand the idea that Jimmy had gotten over her, or worse, simply forgotten her.

After their falling-out, Kay had expected Jimmy to send an angry letter or two, or, at a minimum, make several angry phone calls with the obligatory threats toward Innocent #2. But Jimmy had given her no satisfaction whatsoever. He simply disappeared.

And even worse, her mom and Jimmy's mom had become friends, and Mrs. Sunday preferred Jimmy to her boyfriend and had no problem telling her so.

Innocent #2, for his trouble, had no better option than to detach as Kay became more and more distant. The high-octane sessions fizzled out and left them on the porch lying on separate sofas, staring aimlessly with headaches.

* * * * *

Kay Sunday had had enough harmony. She rose from her sofa, went inside, picked up the phone, and dialed the Branhoovers' number.

Chloe Branhoover answered.

"Hi, Mrs. Branhoover. This is Kay. Is Jimmy there?"

"Oh hello, Kay. My goodness, how have you been? It's been so long," said Chloe Branhoover, looking over her shoulder, hoping her son didn't hear her.

"Not so well," said Kay. "I miss Jimmy. Is he there?"

Though Chloe desperately wanted to lie, she did not. "One moment," she said like a maid, and went to fetch her son.

"Hello?" said Jimmy, with forced nonchalance.

"I miss you, Jimmy," Kay blurted out. "What are you doing? I want to see you."

Kay's directness eviscerated Jimmy's resolve. "Okay," said Jimmy, "let's go hang out with my new friends Charles and Betsy."

Just as he uttered the words "new friends," he heard the voice of Innocent #2 say, "Are you talking to Jimmy Branhoover?" His ears heard the voice, clear and true, but his eyes weren't there to see Innocent #2 shrug and exit out the front door of the Sundays' house.

"You guys must be really bored with each other if the most interesting thing you can come up with is to fuck with me three years later."

"He just left, Jimmy. We're through. We broke up. I want to put on a nice dress and go with you to meet Charles and Betsy."

"I'm sorry, Kay, but I don't believe you. Or I do believe you, but you'll just change your mind tomorrow or an hour from now. Please don't call me again," said Jimmy, and he hung up the phone.

54. Her Son's Intensity

"James, I'm so proud of you," said Chloe Branhoover, who had eavesdropped on the entire phone call.

"You were listening?" asked Jimmy, doing his best to conceal the agony of denying himself the thing he wanted even more than saving a drunkard's life.

His mother hugged him while his mind repeated the words "I want to put on a nice dress and go with you to meet Charles and Betsy," which seemed to knock the wind out of him.

"Thanks," he said, and pulled away from her embrace. "Does the name Betsy Sullivan sound familiar?"

Chloe Branhoover paused, her eyes searching the space in front of her and inside of her.

"Why do I feel that it should?" she said.

"Because Betsy Sullivan dated my brother in high school," said Jimmy. "And now she's dating my old friend you haven't met. They're both nurses."

"Oh, of course. What was I thinking?" said Chloe, laughing with the intention of diffusing her son's intensity.

Jimmy laughed in reply. Then he spoke at length about the rows of destitute men, how his old friend had once been a nameless skid row alcoholic, how he had called Jimmy "Angel," how Jimmy had saved him, how he now had a name (Charles Larson) and a job (nurse) and a girlfriend (Betsy Sullivan), and how Jimmy had spent his fifteenth birthday in their company.

"You really got to know this man, then," said Mrs. Branhoover. She was relieved to finally know the whole truth but was nevertheless alarmed. "Well, I suppose I should tell you that I've been corresponding with your brother since your father died. He would like to meet you, James," she said.

"Where is he? Is he here? In Pittsburgh?" asked Jimmy.

"He lives in New Orleans. Let's go buy you a car so you can visit him," said Chloe with gritty excitement in her voice.

55. A New Car

H. James Branhoover introduced his mother to Charles Larson aka the honest man, and reintroduced her to Betsy Sullivan. The two women sat in the front seat of Betsy's car exchanging war stories about the teenage Bernard Branhoover aka Bernrd Red, while Betsy drove the four of them to the Mercedes dealer.

Jimmy and Charles sat in the backseat in silence, both of them feeling grateful and holy.

In the troubled lives of these four people—Charles Larson the skid row bum, Betsy Sullivan the fussy wet salami, Chloe Red the roughhouse prostitute, and H. James Branhoover the trust fund baby—their morning at the Mercedes dealer was blissfully devoid of adverse truths.

They slid in and out of a dozen or so automobiles and, thanks to the late H. Charles Branhoover, didn't concern themselves with the formidable sticker prices.

Jimmy ultimately decided on a white S500, which his mother purchased in her own name and with her own inheritance.

Charles Larson wept joyously in the backseat of the new car as Mrs. Branhoover drove the four of them off the lot and back to their lives.

56. Lunch with the Branhoovers

Charles Larson looked as though he had just arrived on the summit of Mount Olympus as Jimmy's new Mercedes pulled into the Branhoovers' driveway. He walked to the edge of the property and watched the Allegheny River move through the city, while Jimmy, Chloe, and Betsy went inside to prepare a late lunch. He shivered when he thought about how the quiet man and the inveterate grifter were still down there, either along the rows of destitute men or dead. He recalled how Jimmy had sat with him through his last hangover and how he had not taken a drink since. Then he turned and walked into his angel's mansion to join his friends for lunch.

The conversation focused exclusively on Jimmy's pending trip to New Orleans to meet his brother for the first time.

Chloe Branhoover guaranteed her son that she would teach him all he would need to know about how to drive his new car, and she displayed a refreshingly cavalier attitude about Jimmy being too young to drive and not being able to get a driver's license.

Charles and Betsy were similarly optimistic in this regard, and were positively joyous over the prospect of Jimmy finally meeting his brother.

But then, as if she were sitting at the table, Jimmy heard Kay's voice: "I want to put on a nice dress and go with you to meet your brother."

"I'm thinking about inviting Kay Sunday," Jimmy announced.

Mrs. Branhoover grimaced. "James, how many times do I have to remind you that Kay . . ."

"Ha! I knew you had a girlfriend," said Betsy Sullivan. "Kay what? 'Sunday' did you say? That's kind of odd. Sounds made-up."

"It is made-up," said Jimmy, pleased that Betsy had interrupted his mother. "Her parents are on the eccentric side. Their real last name is Sutter."

"This day just keeps on getting better and better," said Charles Larson. "Of course you must invite her, Angel."

"You sly devil," said Betsy Sullivan.

Chloe Branhoover smiled, rose from her chair, brought her plate into the kitchen, dropped it in the sink, and then returned to the table to announce that lunch was over and how nice it was to have spent the day with Jimmy's wonderful friends.

"Uh-oh," said Betsy.

"Oh, it's not that," said Chloe. "It's just that I am exhausted. I'd love to spend more time with both of you," she said, sincerely.

"This is one of the finest days I can remember," said Charles Larson, rising from his chair, "and it's been a pleasure to spend it in your company."

By now, all four of them were standing. They walked together out to Betsy's car and said goodbye.

57. An Invitation

"James," said Chloe Branhoover as they stepped back inside the house, "if you want to invite Kay to go with you to meet Bernard, then I support you. Anyway, it'll be safer to have company on such a long trip."

Jimmy stared at her for several seconds, still surprised by how different she seemed. "I appreciate that, thanks," he said, and then he picked up the phone and called the Sundays.

"Hello?" said Kay Sunday. The good fireflies stirred to life inside Jimmy's stomach.

"Hi, Kay. It's Jimmy Branhoover. I haven't stopped thinking about you since we last spoke. I'd like to invite you to go with me to New Orleans to meet my big brother. I have a brand-new car and everything. It's a Mercedes S500. White. I just bought it today," he said, laughing nervously.

Kay began to cry. "You've always been such a sweet boy, and I'm sorry for all the times I've been mean to you," she said. "We were childhood friends, and I'll never forget you. I heard how you helped the homeless man. I think you're going to be important, Jimmy. No. You already are important. I love you and I'll never forget you. Goodbye." And she hung up before Jimmy could reply.

He instinctively redialed the number but hung up before it rang.

Kay was right. They were childhood friends and the time of their relationship was over.

Jimmy walked slowly to his bedroom and lay down on the bed. How can I fail to acknowledge the miracle? he thought.

58. A Cryptic Message

At four o'clock in the morning, the Branhoovers' phone rang. Both Chloe and Jimmy thought it was Kay Sunday, but each reacted differently: the irritated Chloe rolled over in bed and covered her ears with a pillow, while the pouncing kitten in Jimmy returned. He sprang upon the phone with childish exuberance, but it was too late. The machine had picked up the call.

Jimmy looked at the clock on the wall and waited five minutes before he lifted the receiver to check messages.

"You have one new message and no saved messages," reported the voicemail service. "To listen to your message, press one."

H. James Branhoover pressed the button.

"First new message . . ."

"Hello, James. This is Vander Stevenson. You've been on my mind a lot lately, which is unusual, believe me. Usually I'm what's on my mind. Ha-ha! You're a good and powerful young man, James. In my experience, those two traits rarely go together. Now, hear me out. Don't ask how—you mustn't ask how—but I know about all of the good and powerful things you've done. Not just for the Sundays, but all of the other things, too. You can do so much more, James. Bigger moths need bigger flames. I think you should leave Pittsburgh. Go somewhere bigger. New York or Chicago. Or Hollywood! Think of the good you could do in Hollywood. You could be famous, James. Bigger moths need bigger flames."

"To delete this message, press seven. To save it, press nine," reported the voicemail service.

Jimmy pressed nine, then replayed the message the number of times it took him to transcribe it verbatim in his notebook.

He returned to his room and lay awake well into the morning, reminiscing about Kay and adjusting the itinerary of his pending trip to include Hollywood.

59. An Inconsequential Lie

"Was that Kay who called at four in the morning?" asked Mrs. Branhoover, carrying a breakfast tray into her son's room.

"Yeah," answered Jimmy. "She said she wanted to tell me she loved me before I left on my trip."

"At that hour? Well, she certainly is beguiling," said Mrs. Branhoover, without irony.

"Oh, now you see it," said Jimmy, laughing. "I'm getting really excited about my trip, Mom, but I'm nervous about meeting Bernard. What if he doesn't like me?"

"Honestly, James, he probably won't like you but if he kicks you out, you've got lots of money and a brand-new car to bring you back home."

"How long will it take to learn how to drive?" asked Jimmy.

"Probably a week or two," said Mrs. Branhoover.

PART VIII

60. From the Ohio to the Mississippi

Eleven days later, H. James Branhoover was—in his mother's estimation—properly trained and ready for his trip. She helped him pack and load the trunk and backseat of the Mercedes, and she hugged him goodbye with a lightness that suggested she expected to see him again soon.

Jimmy took a leisurely five days following the Ohio River west to the Mississippi River and the Mississippi River south to New Orleans, driving cautiously and expertly, and drawing exactly no attention from state troopers from Pennsylvania to Louisiana.

When he arrived in New Orleans, he booked a room in the Riverfront Hilton, where he stayed for a week going on sightseeing tours and walking the streets of the French Quarter, deliberately passing by his brother's address on Toulouse several times.

On the eighth day, he passed by just before sunset and saw a thirty-five-year-old version of himself step out onto his front porch in pajamas, a benign scowl on his face.

61. You Must Be James

"Come here, bro. Let me get a closer look at you," said the scowling man in pajamas.

Jimmy pointed at himself, looking sheepishly to and fro.

"Yes, you," said the scowling man.

Jimmy felt himself scowl a bit as he approached the man directly.

"Blond hair, brown eyes, regal nose. All the traits of a Branhoover. You must be James," said the man.

Jimmy smiled. "And you must be Hugh What's-His-Name? Hefner," he said, trying to break the ice.

"No, I'm his cantankerous and celibate brother, Bernrd," said Bernrd Red, breaking it once and for all.

"BERN-erd? Not BernARD?"

"Didn't Mom tell you? I removed the 'a' from my name," said the Branhoovers' firstborn.

"Yeah, but that was, what, twenty years ago? I thought things might have changed since Pittsburgh," said Jimmy, surprised by his own brazenness.

"You're lucky I'm on my meds," said Bernrd Red, laughing. "Otherwise I'd probably clock you."

Suddenly Jimmy became aware of the music emanating from his brother's apartment, and how it seemed responsible for his cavalier attitude.

"What's that music?" he asked.

"That's Professor Longhair. Why don't you come inside and have a beer with me, James."

"I'd love to," said Jimmy.

The two brothers spent the rest of the evening and into the early morning hours of the next day getting acquainted through music and beer, the latter of which Jimmy liked so much, it made him sick.

62. Much Better Than Gasoline Fumes

The following afternoon, Bernrd Red—wearing the same pajamas as the day before—stumbled into the bathroom and discovered his little brother curled up in his underwear next to the toilet. He prodded Jimmy with his foot to see if the boy was still capable of movement. Jimmy squirmed and rolled over, banging his knees against the bathtub with enough force to startle him awake and into a sitting position.

"It's alive!" said Bernrd Red.

Jimmy managed a weary grin.

"Well, if it turns out everything else about you is contemptible, at least I know you like good beer."

"It's much better than gasoline fumes," Jimmy replied, "but I'm never drinking that much again."

"Ha!" exclaimed Bernrd Red. "Once an alcoholic, always an alcoholic."

"What did you say? 'Ha!?' That reminds me of your ex-girlfriend," said Jimmy.

"I haven't had an *ex*-girlfriend since high school," said Bernrd Red.

"Right," said Jimmy. "Her name is Betsy Sullivan. And I'm not an alcoholic. I do know one, though. I helped him off skid row. Actually, he's Betsy's new boyfriend. They're both nurses."

"Whoa, whoa, stop it, Mother Teresa. Quit being such a bore. I think I like you better when you're drunk."

Jimmy closed his eyes and rubbed his temples, feeling wounded by his brother's failure to be impressed. "Sorry, man. I feel like shit," he said.

"You need something to eat," said Bernrd Red. "Do you like cheeseburgers?"

"I love cheeseburgers," said Jimmy.

So Branhoover the elder escorted Branhoover the younger into the kitchen for microwaved sliders, Pepsi, and a shot of bourbon, and then sent him to bed to sleep off his first hangover.

63. The Worst Thing You've Ever Done

Jimmy woke the following morning feeling much better about everything. His hangover was gone, and his brother wasn't such a bad guy after all— or at least he wasn't as evil as Betsy and his mom had made him out to be.

In fact, even as Jimmy was thinking benevolent thoughts about his brother, Bernrd Red was in the kitchen frying up bacon, eggs, and hash browns for the two of them.

"Breakfast is served, James," the elder Branhoover announced from the stove.

Jimmy met him at the dining room table, where he was surprised to see that the breakfast beverage wasn't tea or orange juice, but beer.

"That's how we do it in New Orleans," said Bernrd Red, reading the concerned expression on Jimmy's face.

"Cool," said Jimmy, taking a healthy swig as a pledge of allegiance to his brother's city.

"Doubtless, Mom has told you some terrible things about me," said Bernrd Red. "Let me assure you that everything she told you is true, and that any of the more far-fetched rumors can be more or less substantiated."

"What's the worst thing you've ever done?" asked Jimmy, without flinching.

"Ha!" exclaimed Bernrd Red. "I definitely like you better when you're drunk."

"I'm not drunk," said Jimmy.

"That's what you think," said Bernrd Red. "Worst thing I've ever done is sleep with a pregnant woman during her honeymoon with another man. Even worse, she wanted me to rough her up and I indulged her."

"Holy crap, you're going to burn in Hell," said Jimmy, laughing.

"What about you, kiddo?" said Bernrd Red.

"Kiddo? I think you need another beer. And you don't have to call me James, either. I know we're Branhoovers and all, but you can call me Jimmy."

"I'll call you whatever I please, Jimmy," said Bernrd Red, wild-eyed and grinning. "And what's the worst thing you've ever done, little brother?"

"I spray-painted the side of a church once," said Jimmy, sheepishly.

"Not bad," said Bernrd Red, confident that he had reestablished his dominance. "What did it say, Jimmy?"

"It was the anti-Simple Prayer. I took St. Francis of Assisi's Simple Prayer, and I made it say the opposite. For example: 'Lord Satan, make me an instrument of Thy chaos. Where there is hatred, let me be called among the haters; where there is injury, let my wrath be the cause; where there is doubt, let me be the spreader of lies,' and so on. I got caught and had to spend the night in jail."

Bernrd Red laughed respectfully. "That's actually pretty twisted," he said.

"Now it's my turn again," said Jimmy. "I've been wondering where you got that ring. Is that a real ruby?"

"It is indeed a real ruby. Do you like it? Of course you do. The ring was a gift. The owner of the Golden Horseshoe in Las Vegas gave it to me for my services as a cooler. Do you know what a cooler is, Jimmy?"

"Uh-uh," said the younger Branhoover, cracking open another beer.

"A cooler is someone who can make a lucky person's good luck turn sour," said Bernrd Red.

Jimmy's mind flashed to the sourness he felt when his brother had called him a bore for helping Charles Larson. Then he thought about Vander Stevenson aka the Reverend Patchouli Goldwatch.

"Oh, crap," said Jimmy. "I've got to check out of my hotel room. I completely forgot about it. I'll come back tonight, if that's okay with you."

"Ha! Forgets he's renting a luxury hotel room. Such a trust fund baby. You're welcome to stay here as long as you want, Jimmy. You're my brother."

Jimmy guzzled the rest of his beer and walked out the door toward the Riverfront Hilton.

64. The Best Thing That Ever Happened to Me

In true brotherly fashion, a week went by before Jimmy showed up again at Bernrd Red's apartment. Also befitting of brothers, Bernrd Red was utterly unconcerned by Jimmy's failure to return and made absolutely no effort to contact him.

H. James Branhoover arrived at his brother's apartment on a Wednesday night carrying a twelve-pack and under the mistaken impression that Bernrd Red had a job and might not want to drink beers with him on a work night.

"A job?" Bernrd Red snorted, again in pajamas. "Why would I have a job? Do you want to know the best thing that ever happened to me . . . to us?"

"What's that?" asked Jimmy.

"That Dad died and made us rich, that's what. You get to drive down here in a new

Mercedes-Benz to hang out with your independently wealthy, happily unemployed, pajama-wearing brother, and we get to sit around and do whatever we please. I mean, you're not even in school, are you?"

"No," said Jimmy, embarrassed.

"Hey, we've got nothing to be ashamed of. You've got your whole life to go to school, if that's what you want. But you get to do it on your own time and not because you need a degree to get some lame job. So let's hang out."

Jimmy handed his brother a beer out of the twelve-pack, opened one for himself, and stepped inside his brother's apartment.

"I don't want to go to school," said Jimmy.

"Good for you, kiddo," said Bernrd Red, challenging his brother to respond.

Jimmy winced. The word "cooler" flashed in his mind, but he managed to stay on topic.

"I'm going to Hollywood," he said.

"Now you're talking," said Bernrd Red. "You're going to be a famous actor, bro."

"Nothing like that," replied Jimmy. "I'm going to help drunks get off skid row. I seem to have a knack for it, and it makes me feel good."

"It's just one drunk talking to another drunk. Isn't that the cliché?"

"You *are* a fucking cooler," said Jimmy.

"Hey, man, if you can't handle the beer, then you're going to have to leave," said Bernrd Red, calmly and condescendingly.

"That's okay by me," said Jimmy. "It was good meeting you."

"Well, at least this isn't a story about a boy and his dog," said the elder Branhoover, who stood and showed his little brother to the door.

65. An Inconsequential Lie

Jimmy returned to his room at the Riverfront Hilton and wrote the following letter:

Dear Mom:

The trip to New Orleans was a success. "BERNrd" is difficult, just like you said he would be. I think he's some kind of ruby-ring voodoo priest in pajamas. But he didn't kick me out until tonight.

I have decided to head to Hollywood to try acting. Please don't worry. The idea was mine, not Bernrd's, and I promise to stay away from skid row.

The car is running great. I miss you and hope you are doing well.

–Jimmy

P.S. Say "Hi" to Charles and Betsy if you see them.

PART IX

66. From the Riverfront Hilton to the Beverly Hilton

Jimmy's 1,900-mile journey from New Orleans to Los Angeles after his falling-out with Bernrd Red reminded him of his eight-mile walk from the Sundays' porch to the rows of destitute men after his falling-out with Kay Sunday.

For 1,900 miles Jimmy drove expertly in his Mercedes-Benz, reflecting on the events of his recent past.

The more time and distance away from his brother, the more disturbing he found their visit to be. Bernrd Red seemed to possess a pernicious energy that was best gotten away from. Maybe he *was* a voodoo priest.

And what of the cryptic message left by Vander Stevenson aka the Reverend Patchouli Goldwatch? Jimmy had transcribed the message verbatim, but part of him wondered whether the call was real or a figment of his four-in-the-morning imagination. Maybe it *was* just a late-night hang-up. Or maybe Kay was right and Goldwatch was the Devil himself.

And what of Kay Sunday? The more time and distance away from Kay, the more his mind focused on her attractive aspects and disregarded the rest: "You've always been such a sweet boy, and I'm sorry for all the times I've been mean to you" and "We were childhood friends, and I'll never forget you" and "You already are important. I love you and I'll never forget you." Jimmy couldn't help but wonder how different things might be if she were sitting next to him now.

And what of his mother? Chloe Red the roughhouse prostitute had accomplished what the vast majority of human beings are incapable of or otherwise flat-out refuse to do: she had changed for the better. In fact, Jimmy wondered at the wisdom of her allowing him to make his own decisions. Shouldn't he be in school? Shouldn't he have waited until he was of legal age before driving across the country? Shouldn't he be afraid to lie to her? Jimmy's answer to each of these questions was yes. He vowed that he would never lie to her again.

* * * * *

While his trip from Pittsburgh to New Orleans took a leisurely five days (probably out of fear of meeting his brother), his journey to Los Angeles was decidedly more urgent.

H. James Branhoover traveled from the Riverfront Hilton to the Beverly Hilton in four days. He checked into his top-floor suite, showered, wrapped himself in the Beverly Hilton's signature bathrobe, laughed because it reminded him of his brother in his pajamas, took it off, lay on the king-size bed, and fell asleep on top of the comforter with the lights on.

67. A Successful Bribe

The next afternoon, H. James Branhoover discovered Trader Vic's. He planted himself in a booth and successfully bribed the waitress to serve him mai tais.

He heard his brother's voice: "Once an alcoholic, always an alcoholic." He dismissed it as more pernicious voodoo. How could a fifteen-year-old be an alcoholic? Charles Larson—now he was an alcoholic. And what of it? If all alcoholics were like me and Charles Larson, then there should be more of us, he thought.

He ordered another mai tai, his fifth, and thought fond thoughts about everybody and everything. Then he curled up in the booth and passed out. The waitress revived him and snuck him outside.

Jimmy awoke in his bed at two in the morning, the day's events erased completely from his mind.

68. A Confession

Jimmy sat in his suite in the Beverly Hilton and wrote the following letter:

Dear Mom:

I have arrived safely in Los Angeles. I'm staying at the Beverly Hilton. I confess that I have lied to you twice.

The first time was when the phone rang at four in the morning. It wasn't Kay Sunday on the line. It was Vander Stevenson, the man who bought the Sundays' church. And actually, now that I have some distance between now and then, I'm not sure it was him either. The message he left for me was so strange that I can't help but wonder if my imagination got the best of me at that early hour. It could be that I was just very stressed about meeting Bernrd, and the call was nothing but a hang-up. Please don't be alarmed. I don't mean to scare you with this news, though I can understand if you find it troubling.

The second time was when I told you I was coming to Hollywood to try acting and that I would stay away from skid row. The truth is that I have no interest in acting, and the real reason I came here is to volunteer at the homeless shelters and missions on, well, skid row. You met Charles Larson. He was a skid row bum, and I helped him get out of there. I'm not pursuing an education—at least not yet—so for now I think this is what I'm supposed to do.

I apologize for telling you these lies. I understand that you have entrusted me to make my own decisions and that you're being lenient with me because you don't want me to wind up like Bernrd. So, no more lies from me.

–Jimmy

69. A Living Entry

As Jimmy tore the page containing the letter from his notebook, he discovered a strand of Kay Sunday's long blonde hair among the pages, no doubt from the time of the high-octane sessions.

This is a living entry, he thought. Then he wrote the following words: "Church blonde. Mother hen blonde. Pretty blonde. Wholesome. Winsome. Helpful."

Jimmy stared at his entry vis-à-vis Kay's hair for a good long minute, feeling perplexed and nostalgic. He closed the notebook on the page of this entry using the strand as a sort of bookmark.

This calls for a mai tai, he thought. He dressed himself accordingly and went down to Trader Vic's, where he was promptly informed by management that he had been eighty-sixed from the premises and that, thanks to him, the waitress who served him had been fired.

And so went the next two years, in a haze of mai tais and blackouts and beers, never setting foot on the rotting pavement of skid row, but often opening his notebook to look at the living entry.

70. Eighteenth Birthday

Around the time of his eighteenth birthday, Jimmy received a card and a letter signed by his mom, Charles Larson, and Betsy Sullivan, wishing him a happy birthday, reminding him that he was now old enough to vote, saying that all was well in the city of Pittsburgh, hoping that his work with the homeless in Los Angeles was going as well as it did in his hometown, and announcing that Charles and Betsy were moving in together.

This was Jimmy's first experience with that troubling phenomenon of time—how two years can slip away unnoticed, how they can get behind you and sneak out the back door with your plans, goals, dreams, and best intentions.

The birthday letter shocked Jimmy into action. He began cruising the streets of downtown Los Angeles in his Mercedes, ten thousand dollars in the glove box, scanning the faces of the destitute men and women in search of an apt beneficiary.

Several days passed without result, and Jimmy began to grow impatient. He needed something to report back home, but he no longer seemed to have the will or, perhaps more accurately, the desperation, to interact with down-and-out and often mentally unstable human beings.

So, on a late afternoon approximately two weeks after his eighteenth birthday, H. James Branhoover drank several beers and promised himself that this would be the day he changed someone's life.

He drove east on Wilshire Boulevard into downtown Los Angeles, which quickly disintegrates into skid row. He scanned the faces of the men and women fidgeting in filthy rows, looking into their eyes for an indication that they had not abandoned God.

Finally, he saw a man who reminded him of Charles Larson, though much older and far weaker. He leapt out of the car, put the ten thousand dollars into the bewildered man's coat pocket, and mumbled something about jobs through Goodwill and getting an apartment. Then he returned to the car, drove straight ahead for several blocks, made a U-turn, and headed back to the spot of his philanthropy.

The elderly man whose eyes had not abandoned God lay coatless and dead in an expanding pool of his own blood. Jimmy instinctively kept driving west through downtown, onto Wilshire Boulevard, and eventually back to his suite in the Beverly Hilton, his body seemingly on the verge of total organ failure.

He lay in bed for what could've been two hours or two days with the singular and unrelenting thought that the only way he could ever find relief would be to kill himself.

71. Divorced

Sometime later in his changed days, H. James Branhoover packed his belongings and checked out of the Beverly Hilton. He drove and lived in his car, divorced from the city and in a black state of mind.

Every moment of his life preceding the skid row incident had been erased. His mother and father, Kay Sunday, Innocent #2 and the Reverend Patchouli Goldwatch, Mrs. Germany, Charles Larson and Betsy Sullivan, the quiet man and the inveterate grifter, his brother, the anti-

Simple Prayer: all gone. He was no longer among the living, but he was not yet among the dead.

Eventually the living intruded.

The Mercedes had been parked for two days on Santa Monica Boulevard near Cherokee Avenue in Hollywood. This caught the attention of the boys who fake gayness for the sake of slavery, who tapped on the windshield to get Jimmy's attention.

For reasons of youth, ignorance, or otherwise, Jimmy had never been what most people would consider scared during his days with the rows of destitute men. The sight of these three boys, however, none older than fifteen, with stray cat physiques and the fearlessness that comes with a lack of respect for life, terrified him. He pretended to be asleep, but the tapping only grew louder.

"We're not going to hurt you," said the first boy, a practiced effeminacy in his voice.

"Unless you don't talk to us," said the second boy. All three of them laughed.

The laughter flipped a switch in Jimmy's mind. If these three imps jacked his car and left him for dead, the ordeal would be over. This world would no longer concern him. He turned the key in the ignition and rolled down all four windows.

"What do you sweet little boys want?" said Jimmy, tauntingly.

"You!" said the third boy, flashing a mean grin.

"Good, get in then, and let's go," said Jimmy.

The boys glanced at one another, shrugged, and then slid onto the plush leather seats of the Mercedes.

"Do you boys like beer?" asked Jimmy.

"Are you going to get me drunk?" asked the first boy, flirtatiously.

"I'm going to get all of us drunk, and I'm going to pay each of you two thousand dollars for the privilege," said Jimmy.

"Oh, fuck yeah!" said the third boy.

"Where do you boys live?" asked Jimmy.

"Youth hostel on Highland, near the Bowl," said the second boy. "And there's a liquor store just down the street."

72. Six-Thousand-Dollar Promise

H. James Branhoover and the three street boys arrived at the youth hostel with two cases of beer in tow. Jimmy procured a room for himself, good for a year, and invited the boys to join him.

The four of them drank the first case within an hour or two, but no quantity of alcohol could erase Jimmy's six-thousand-dollar promise from the boys' minds.

"So where's our money?" asked the first boy.

This could be it, thought Jimmy. "What money?" he asked.

"You bitch," said the first boy, clearly acting as spokesman for the other two. "The two thousand for each of us."

"Oh, that was a lie. I thought you were savvy enough to know better," said Jimmy, wincing in anticipation of extreme violence.

To Jimmy's surprise, however, the boys seemed to lose their impish quality. Now they very much appeared as they truly were: frightened teenage runaways. The mood in Jimmy's new room changed entirely.

"I'm sorry," said Jimmy, reaching into the second case and tossing each boy a fresh beer. "I was kind of hoping to die tonight and thought you might be able to help me."

"Nah, we're not killers," said the second boy.

"We're trying to die too," said the third boy, still grinning.

"What's the worst thing you've ever done?" asked Jimmy, on the brink of telling the boys about the skid row incident.

"Let's get out of here," said the first boy.

"Yeah, let's go," said the second boy.

All three boys stood, downed their beers, and tossed the cans to the floor.

"Aren't you coming with us?" asked the third boy, still grinning.

And the four new acquaintances walked out of the youth hostel and into the heart of Hollywood, drunk and trying to forget the worst things they'd ever done.

73. Dimmed the Light in Their Eyes

Jimmy spent the next several months in the company of the three street boys, though they never progressed from acquaintances to friends. They couldn't. Living in the youth hostel in the soft prison of Hollywood forbade it and dimmed the light in their eyes.

And Jimmy's participation in the rituals of their acquaintanceship was limited, much as it was during the high-octane sessions with Kay Sunday and Innocent #2. Where the street boys found temporary relief in shoplifting trinkets, conning tourists, and harassing fellow runaways and the homeless, Jimmy found none. His body was present, but he didn't participate. Where Kay and Innocent #2 took comfort in the ritual of inhaling gasoline fumes, Jimmy barely passed the can under his nose.

The alienation he felt on Kay Sunday's porch was nothing compared to that he felt in Hollywood. In Hollywood, he was trying to die. The further in the past the skid row incident, the greater the magnitude of his guilt.

To the boys' delight and amusement, Jimmy became agitated whenever they harassed a homeless man. So much so, in fact, that this became the boys' primary nocturnal activity.

Jimmy saw at least one aspect of the man from the skid row incident in all of the men and women the boys harassed: the style, depth, and character of the skin; the condition of cuts, scrapes, and bruises; the wildness of the hair; the way the eyes had not abandoned God.

But Jimmy didn't protest any amount of taunting, prodding, or other bullying until the night the boys looked down a stretch of pavement between medium buildings just off the Walk of Fame and spotted a man who—like the man downtown—reminded Jimmy of Charles Larson.

The boys pushed up their sleeves, pursed their lips, and started down the alley to do their impish worst, when Jimmy let his head and back thud against the building and his body slide into a seated position on the sidewalk. He covered his eyes with his hands and wept with such force that the boys were compelled to pay attention.

"Whatever is the matter, dear James?" asked the first boy, his voice already locked in feminine mode.

"Please leave that man alone," mumbled Jimmy. "At least when I'm here. Please."

"Look at that!" exclaimed the second boy. "He's finally having a breakdown."

"It's about time," said the third boy, still grinning. "We were starting to think you were some kind of psychopath."

"Sure, we'll leave him alone. Whatever you want, James," said the first boy.

"Hey, let's get some beers and get wasted in Jimmy's room," said the second boy.

Jimmy did his best to compose himself. "Nah, I'm just going to crash tonight," he said, rising from the huddled mass of himself and walking back to his room in the youth hostel, knowing for certain he would never see these boys again.

74. An Adverse Truth and an Inconsequential Lie

Jimmy sequestered himself in his room, seeing no one and going outside only for beer and fast food. Sitting uncomfortably among grease-stained wrappers and twelve-pack carcasses, he composed two letters: one to Charles Larson and the other to his mother.

> *Dear Charles:*
>
> *I know it's been a long time since we've talked, but that doesn't mean I don't think about you. I was delighted to hear that you and Betsy have moved in together. Could marriage be far off?*
>
> *As for me, things are not going well at all. I got a man killed, Charles. I gave him ten grand down on skid row and someone must have seen me do it, because when I returned, his coat was gone and he was dead. I have started thinking about the martyrs, and I*

think I understand how they find the courage to do what they must.

And to make matters even worse, I can't stop drinking. I'm not sure I want to anyway. When I'm wasted, I look in my notebook. But I don't read the words. I know this is probably the epitome of pathetic, but I found a strand of Kay Sunday's hair among the pages, and I just sit there and look at it. It brings me more comfort than the words.

Yours always,

Haley James Branhoover

Dear Mom:

Things aren't going quite as I'd expected here in terms of helping on skid row, but I haven't given up. Also, I've moved out of the Hilton and into a youth hostel. The hotel just seemed like a waste of Dad's money, and I've got some new friends who live a few doors down from me. It's a really good arrangement.

Isn't it wonderful that Charles and Betsy have moved in together? If they get married, I'm definitely coming home for the wedding. Anyway, I just want to say thank you for being such a great mom and for trusting me to make my own decisions.

Love,

James

75. Rancid Words

On a summer evening late in his nineteenth year, Haley James Branhoover, the Branhoovers' second son, stared at the suicide note he had dashed off moments earlier on the heels of a week of heavy drinking, no company, and sporadic sleep.

A part of him wished his final words could have been the letters he had just sent to Charles Larson and his mom. But it was too late for those.

He needed to record his final words here, but he couldn't wait for proper inspiration to strike, because he had the courage to do this now.

He picked the note up off the nightstand and read it aloud:

> *And so I ran away to Hollywood. Bigger moths need bigger flames. I know after I jump off this building, the world will mourn and pandemonium and chaos will reign. For the record, my dad was a good-for-nothing banker and my mom was an abusive whore. Good riddance to them. Didn't they know who I was? Come to think of it, didn't any of you people know who I was? Fuck all of you!*
> *No longer yours,*
> *H. James Branhoover*

The words were rancid. They reeked of pernicious voodoo.

"Trust fund baby," he said.

He set the note back on the nightstand and stared at it again. He couldn't stand the sight of it, so he sealed it in the nearest thing he could find: a business reply envelope for *Playboy* magazine.

He went downstairs to the mailroom and dropped the envelope in the slot. On his way back up, he read the words "Roof Access" around each turn of the staircase.

He walked into the open air on the roof. "Roof Access," he said. He repeated the phrase. It gave him unexpected energy.

He sat down on the edge and dangled his legs over.

76. Dear Angel

On the last day of Jimmy's life, a letter arrived in the mailroom of the Beverly Hilton.

Dear James:

First, the good news. Your kind letter inspired me to propose to Betsy. I had been considering it for months, and then I received your letter. James, she said yes! I'll inform you immediately of the wedding date, and not only do I hope you'll attend, but I would be honored if you would be my best man. Please consider it, James.

And now the further good news. You did not get a man killed. I don't care what the circumstances were. His murder is the fault of those who murdered him, and no one else's. Please don't blame yourself. You are a good man, James, and what you did for that poor soul was even more than good. It was holy.

Oh, dear Angel, how can you fail to acknowledge the miracle?

Yours always,

Charles Larson

Acknowledgments

Special thanks to my editors, Jen Richardson, Laura A. Lionello, and Greg Dalgleish, for their expert guidance in the evolution and completion of this book.

About the Author

Douglas Richardson was born on February 20, 1967, in Duluth, Minnesota, and was raised in Camarillo, California. He currently lives in Los Angeles, where he works as a proofreader, editor, novelist, and poet.

Also by Weak Creature Press:

Ghosts in Time and Space by Douglas Richardson
Richardson's *Ghosts in Time and Space* offers
groundwarmers a luminous triptych of memory,
emotion, and expression, fortified by unique
wisdom borne of experience.
ISBN-10: 0984242449 (paper)
ISBN-13: 978-0-9842424-4-3 (paper)

Panic Kit by Laura A. Lionello
Panic Kit, Laura A. Lionello's breakout collection
of poetry, showcases the author's deft hand and
mastery of voice in dealing with universal themes
and truths, such as joy, heartache, loss, suffering,
and triumph.
ISBN-10: 0984242430 (paper)
ISBN-13: 978-0-9842424-3-6 (paper)

Poems for Loners by Douglas Richardson
In his fourth enigmatic offering, Douglas
Richardson employs poems, lyrics, proverbs,
letters, and a diary to illuminate the dark lives of
loners.
ISBN-10: 0984242422 (paper)
ISBN-13: 978-0-9842424-2-9 (paper)

The Corruption of Zachary R. by Douglas
Richardson
Compunction and collusion drive Zachary R. He
harbors disillusionment even while performing
life's richest rituals: employment, courtship,

marriage, and fatherhood. Memories of a neurotic mother and emotionally austere father shade his adult life with ever-darkening tones. Riddled with madness, he reaches out to those who survive him, those whom he loves, those who will seek to do him harm. Their collective path to sanity is neither uncomplicated nor without redemption. Who among them will survive the journey?

ISBN-10: 0984242414 (paper)
ISBN-13: 978-0-9842424-1-2 (paper)

Out in the Cold, Cold Day by Douglas Richardson
Poetry chapbook offered exclusively through the publisher. (paper)

All titles offered by Weak Creature Press may be purchased directly from the publisher. Please send an email to weakcreature@aol.com for orders or inquiries. Otherwise, you may purchase our titles via online retailers or ask your local bookseller to order them for you.